Advance Praise for
NOVICE MYSTERY – FRANCE

"Masterful misdirection. Don't miss *France!*"

–Avanti Centrae, multi-award-winning and international bestselling author of the VanOps thriller series

"*Novice Mystery – France*, by Donna Rewolinski, is a page-turner. Ms. Rewolinski is an excellent storyteller and masterful writer. From the beginning, she lulls you into a lovely and peaceful setting with a seemingly ordinary couple on vacation—Dan and his wife Karen are in a glass-enclosed riverboat gliding along the Seine River under the afternoon sun. They are enjoying a lovely day and a delicious meal. All seems so perfectly ordinary, and then we learn that their last vacation was in Mexico, where they 'ended up investigating several crimes, including murder.' Pow! I'm turning pages at the speed of light.

"The couple is invited by old friends (Honoré and Michelle) to a murder game in Paris involving guests from around the world. There is a sense of foreboding as the author artfully leads us to recall the 'Masquerade' from *The Phantom of the Opera*. Ms. Rewolinski builds the characters so that the reader feels empathy for them. You will cheer and laugh and, at times, choke up. I did not want the story to end, but I don't think I am giving anything away when I say the ending will leave you with a satisfied smile and looking forward to the next novel by this author. Well done, Ms. Rewolinski."

–Nick Chiarkas, award-winning author of *Weepers* and *Nunzio's Way*

"Dan and Karen Novice are a delightful detective duo who just happen to run into murder wherever they travel. Visiting Paris, they are excited to spend time with friends who offer to show them the capital and a visit to a family winery featuring a murder mystery event, just up the alley for retired policeman Dan and his amateur sleuth wife. Once they arrive at the winery, tensions among the guests and weather culminate in tragedy.

"Paris and France come to life in the descriptions and the food is a wonderful fillip. This is the third book in this delightful series. If you've read the first two, you'll love this engaging entry. And if this is your first encounter with the Novices, you have a treat in store."

–Sharon Michalove, author of the Global Security Unlimited series

"A murder mystery–themed weekend with good friends at the villa of a secluded vineyard in France would be the perfect vacation for Karen and Dan Novice if not for the storm, no phone or internet, and a spate of real murders. At least the food and wine are excellent!"

–G.P. Gottlieb, author of the Whipped and Sipped Mystery series

"*Novice Mystery – France* by Donna Rewolinski pulls you in on an adventure with Karen and Dan in France, which should be a fun, relaxing getaway to celebrate retirement! Their fun adventure quickly turns awry and has you on the edge of your seat during a murder mystery weekend with friends. Rewolinski's writing has you in France eating wonderful food, having drinks with friends, and watching over your back for who is next to go."

–Lauren Guelig, author of *Wish Me a Rainbow*

NOVICE MYSTERY
FRANCE

THE THIRD DAN & KAREN NOVICE MYSTERY

DONNA REWOLINSKI

Ten|16
PRESS

www.ten16press.com - Waukesha, WI

I'd like to thank my husband, Frank, for his love, support, and technical advice. Also, I want to thank Kim Suhr, members of the Thursday night Red Oak Writing critique group, and members of the Blackbird Writers, who have read, edited, reread, and provided guidance through the publishing process.

CHAPTER 1

The afternoon sun sparkles off the Seine River. Our glass-enclosed riverboat glides effortlessly through the water. The October weather has been perfect thus far. Our first two days have been warm and sunny. A live trio in the cabin softly plays upbeat French music. A low din of voices murmurs all around. My wife, Karen, gently rubs her fingertips across the top of my hand as she gazes out the windows.

She points. "Dan, you can see Notre Dame. It's so sad to see it now. I wish we could've seen it before the fire."

"Does that mean the Hunchback is homeless?" I question.

She drops her shoulders and cocks her head at me. "You're naughty, but I hadn't thought of that . . . maybe. I'm glad of the support they've received to help rebuild."

Still being playful, I say, "We'll plan our second trip to Paris when the reconstruction is complete. Maybe they need an assistant for the renovation. You have experience now."

She laughs. "The hacienda in Mexico was a lot of fun. But so much smaller. Notre Dame would take a bit longer." She wiggles her eyebrows at me. "Maybe we should just move here from Watson."

I shake my head from side to side and think back on our

trip last year to Mexico. The plan was to visit old friends, but Karen and I ended up investigating several crimes, including murder, attempted murder, and cattle rustling. We learned about the Chupacabra. She was involved in renovating a Spanish hacienda and catching a murderer. I quietly snicker to myself.

"Here's to a peaceful vacation in France," she says, raising her glass of champagne. I gently clink mine to hers.

"Here's to hoping," I reply.

Her eyes dance. "I'm really looking forward to seeing Honoré and Michelle again. It's been too long."

"It has. Probably five or six years since they visited us in Watson."

"Wow, it's been that long. I know you met in Washington, D.C. about ten years ago, but I can't remember why you were there."

"We attended the Advanced Forensic Investigations school."

The boat has the slightest sway. It lulls and relaxes me as we continue down the river. Our waiter, Lèo, places our first course in front of us. "*Madame. Monsieur. Bon appétit.*" It's a salad of lettuce hearts, cubes of salmon, a large wedge of both mango and avocado, slivers of radishes, and shaved cheese over the top. A dollop of tangy Dijon vinaigrette rests on all four sides of the plate, accompanied with a small crusted top roll and butter. A glass of pinot noir also appears.

Karen has a few sips of her wine. "Will you finish my wine if I don't like it? I'll drink the champagne and, like always, have water." I happily agree.

We tuck into the salad. The flavors blend perfectly. Staff whisk empty plates and glasses off our table while we take in the ever-changing scenery. I love the architecture. Buildings with balconies and hundreds of years of history.

"I'm looking forward to spending time with Michelle. She has the best taste in clothes. She always looks superb. If we go shopping, do you and Honoré plan on coming or doing something else?"

I shrug. "Hadn't really thought about it. I was gonna leave it up to him."

Karen puts her elbows on the table and leans forward with a sly grin. "*No* playing police detectives."

I wink. "Honestly, *that* thought never occurred to me."

"Pfft" escapes her lips.

I throw my hands up and give her my best "What?" look. "I'd like to visit where they live. I know he's the police chief. What's the name of the town?"

"La Devouement. Maybe we could drive out together. Michelle and I could poke around the shops while you two check out the police station. Oh, listen to me. What am I saying?"

I jump on the opening. "Just remember you suggested it, I didn't." I scan the boat and note the other passengers. Old cop habits.

Lèo returns with our second course. "*Excusez-moi.*"

Pork medallions sit atop baby carrots, new potatoes, turnips, and peapods all covered in a sweet apricot glaze. He also pours glasses of chardonnay and refills the water glasses.

"It's really nice of them to take time off to be our guides while we're in Paris," Karen says.

3

"I agree. However, I'm looking forward to the murder mystery event at Michelle's father's winery. Honoré said they'd have more details when we see them."

Karen rolls her eyes. "Great. A vacation with murder already in it." She takes my hand. "I hope we're not imposing on their family."

"Honoré sounded relieved when we accepted the invitation. He's never said much about his in-laws, but I always got the feeling they don't approve of him. So, he may be looking for some support during the week."

"That's too bad. He's a great guy. He and Michelle seem very happy together."

Lèo places a platter of sliced cheeses, grapes, apple wedges, and cashews between us.

Karen glances out the window. "We've passed several places I'd love to see. The Louvre is somewhere I'd like to spend the day. I also want to see the Grand Palais. I know we'd be viewing a great deal of artwork, but I find it fascinating. If we don't get to them now, then we can see them after the party."

Cheese and nuts fill my mouth, so I nod in agreement. Karen snorts a laugh. "I always have a list of places to see, but what about you?"

A quick swig of wine clears my mouth. "Yes, I'd like to see the Arc de Triomphe at night. I bet the city looks spectacular from up there, and a show at the Moulin Rouge sounds fun."

The final course arrives. Karen's eyes light up with delight. It's half of a baked almond meringue, filled with pastry cream, topped with fresh raspberries and blueberries and sliced strawberries. Her first bite causes a pause and a deep "yum." I agree the taste is perfect, especially with a double espresso. I love coffee.

Karen leans back in her chair. "I'm so full, but it was delicious. I'm glad we did this. It's wonderful." She grabs my hand and gives it a squeeze.

I must admit I feel very happy right now. I have the love of my life with me, my health, and good friends to enjoy this with. At the boat docks, passengers stand and move toward the front of the boat. We let others hurry past us. We're on vacation and in no rush. A sudden wave causes one elderly man to trip up the stairs. A member of the crew catches his arm and helps him onto dry land. We're near the Eiffel Tower.

"Let's head to the top," Karen suggests, looking up.

Tickets purchased, we're herded into tiny, caged elevators for the first part, then a second elevator to the top level. I buy a flute of champagne for each of us from the champagne bar. We clink a toast to health, happiness, and another adventure as we gaze out over Paris. I'm beginning to feel the effects of the wine and champagne, but in a good way. A few circles around, a second glass of champagne, and time melts away until we head back down. We stroll along the river. The sun begins to descend, the lights slowly come on, and the city buzzes. Karen asks that we sit at a small café to enjoy a dessert and coffee before continuing.

We order two Nutella-filled crepes with whipped cream and coffees. Karen asks, "This weekend at Michelle's father's house is a murder mystery weekend, but doesn't that seem like a strange birthday party theme for a man turning eighty-five years old?"

"Honoré said that his father-in-law chooses a different theme every five years. It was *Alice in Wonderland* once."

Karen frowns. "That seems an odd choice for an older person. He must be a very interesting man. I can hardly wait to meet him."

We finish and walk to the Arc de Triomphe. Tickets are purchased, and we begin the climb. Stone steps and narrow stairwells interspersed with landings until we reach the top.

Karen puts her hands on her hips and breathes deeply. "I think we just climbed five thousand steps."

I shake my head. "I read in a guidebook that it's only 284."

"Of course you read it. Well, it felt like five thousand," she replies laughingly.

"Maybe we should have taken the elevator and then walked the remaining sixty-four steps," I say.

Karen narrows her eyes and focuses on me. "There was an elevator? Now you tell me."

I bite my lip. We wander around the top. It is an amazing city by night.

Armed guards are positioned at every corner, and fencing surrounds the edges of the roof. No one wants a suicide or an act of terrorism. Cop habits die hard: I always assess my surroundings. The city twinkles with lights. We stroll all four sides on this fabulous autumn evening. The continuous car headlights and taillights weave ribbons of red and white around the Arc. Traffic seems to be a nightmare; I'm glad I don't have to drive in it. We slowly make our way down, reading plaques that outline the history of the building as we go. Luckily, they are in both French and English. The building was originally designed to be a giant elephant, but that design was denied. I'm not sure

I'd be willing to climb to the belly of a large pachyderm. This structure was completed in 1836. Under the Arc is France's Tomb of the Unknown Soldier from World War I, along with an eternal flame that inspired Jackie Kennedy to have one for her husband upon his death. This is my kind of interesting: duty, honor, and sacrifice. I'm holding Karen's hand in this beautiful city and know I'm truly a lucky person.

We start a slow walk, arm in arm, to our hotel.

"It has been such a magical night. We could be in the movie *Midnight in Paris*. If an antique car with people dressed in twenties-style clothing pulls up and asks us to join them, we're getting in," Karen remarks.

"Without question," I agree. It's one of my favorite romantic movies. Tonight, I believe it could happen.

Minutes later, we arrive. We make our way through the lobby and decide to stop in the hotel bar for a drink. The room is empty, and we sit at the bar. The bartender, Adam, greets us. "*Salut*, what can I get you?"

I order a pastis with a glass of ice on the side. Karen chooses a French 75. Our drinks arrive, and we chat happily with Adam, who wants to practice his English. We discover he is working his way through the university, studying business. We order another round and talk about our trip planned for the winery, and nearly an hour and a half passes. Karen touches my arm. "I think I need to get some sleep."

We thank Adam for an enjoyable evening, pay our bill, and collect our belongings. When we turn to leave, he calls out, "When at the winery, beware the *Feu Follet*."

"The what?" I ask.

Adam smiles. "It is something my grandmother would say. *Feu* means 'fire' and *Follet is* 'spirit.' *Feu Follet* is a soul sent back from the dead. He attacks people for vengeance."

"What does he or she look like, so I know who to avoid?" Karen questions.

"It's not a person, but more a ghostly light that flickers. Do not follow the lights as that leads you to your death."

"Much like the Irish will-o'-the-wisp. Thanks for the warning." I smile and wave to him. I flash back to our vacation in Ireland when will-o'-the-wisps led Karen and I to Lord O'Connor's body. Not something I want to repeat.

We make our way up the winding staircase that leads to the second floor and our room. I unlock and push open the door. Karen stops in her tracks.

"What's wrong?" I ask, trying to look around her.

"Nothing." Karen sighs. "I love this hotel. Our room is perfect."

I laugh as I nudge Karen into the room.

Karen's eyes scan the room. A big bed, a glass chandelier, rose-patterned curtains, French doors that open and allow us to look out onto Paris. The bathroom is decadent with a claw-foot tub, porcelain fixtures, and a handheld shower hose.

"I feel very bourgeoisie. Is that bad to say in Paris?" Karen asks, cocking her head to one side.

I reply in my best French accent, "If this were the 1790s, madame, I would say yes, as we would end up having a date with the guillotine."

"Well, I'm off to soak in a hot bath as a nightcap to this wonderful day. Thank you for it all." She kisses my cheek.

"Thank you for sticking with me through my career." I change, slip into bed, and hear the water running as I fall asleep. If this is what hard work buys, it was worth every moment of it.

CHAPTER 2

Morning breaks gray with low-hanging angry clouds. We decide to have a low-key day in anticipation of our friends' arrival. The morning is spent reading and napping. We finish eating a late lunch in the hotel bar when I receive a text. "Honoré says they're just about here."

"Perfect. We can meet them in the lobby."

A few minutes later, I see our old friends. Honoré's hair—previously thick, black, and wavy—is now streaked with white and thinned, but his waistline has increased. His smile is as brilliant as I remember. I reach my hand out to shake his, but he grabs me and kisses me on each cheek. "*Mon ami*, it has been too long. You look well." He beams down at me.

"Y-You too." I stammer, stepping back and looking up at him.

He slaps his belly. "The price of good French food." He lets out a roar of laughter.

Karen and Michelle are hugging and giggling. Michelle is beautiful—petite, with her black hair swept up into a soft bun and a blue dress tailored to her curves. Michelle hugs me while Honoré kisses Karen's cheeks.

"It is good of both of you to come," Honoré says. "Are you ready for this weekend?"

I reply, "We're packed and settled with the hotel."

"*Parfait*. Michelle and I will drive you to her father's country home."

Karen replies, "That sounds wonderful. We can catch up in the car."

Honoré nods. "*Oui*. Let us go. It is about a two-hour drive."

Karen and I retrieve our luggage from the front desk. It's a short walk to the car. A very nice car. The Peugeot 508. A four-door black sedan. Great ride. Honoré slaps me on the back and winks. I can't help but smile. Luggage goes in the trunk, and we're on our way. Karen and Michelle sit in the back to talk.

Honoré and Michelle don't have any children, but do ask about Eric, our son, and his family.

"They're really busy. They had hoped to join us, but Megan is four months pregnant, and with two small children, travel is difficult," Karen replies.

Michelle gushes, "Three grandchildren. I am so happy for you. Give them my best when you talk to them."

"Thank you. That's very kind of you. I'll let them know," Karen says. "Not to change the subject, but about this party. Honoré, you said it's a murder mystery theme?"

Honoré states. "*Oui*. My father-in-law's name is Oliver Bres. He is an international businessman with many interests. He has been very secretive about these plans." He shoots a glance at Michelle.

"Honoré is trying to say that my father is very wealthy and that this will be a big affair," Michelle adds.

Karen looks at Michelle but can't see Honoré's expression from behind. "Are you sure your father wants us there?"

"Oh, yes," Honoré cuts in. "He said he wants a 'real' detective there. He knew about our trip to visit you. He asked for you both."

I stare out the window, and my thoughts wander. Why Karen and me? Honoré's career has been law enforcement. Why is that not enough? Does he not think much of him or that both of us will be stumped? Curiouser and curiouser. Should I be wary of my host's intentions? I wonder what Karen thinks and feels about meeting this man.

Two fingers tap my left shoulder. "Dan?"

"I'm sorry. I wasn't listening."

"Michelle was telling us some of the plans. This party sounds amazing. Her father has invited a number of associates from around the world to join us." I notice Honoré nodding in agreement.

Michelle blushes. "*Oui*. My father has said that this will be his last big birthday party, as well as his retirement. I think my father will give his company to my brother to run. My mother died four years ago, and my father seemed lost for a while. He gained weight and was very angry, depressed, and focused only on making more money."

Karen lays her hand on Michelle's arm. "I'm so sorry. We never knew your mother had passed."

"My father wanted the service small and private—no outside people knew or attended—but I should have told you."

Honoré cuts in. "The good news is that he seems better. How you say, 'a vigor for life'? He has started eating organic, has slimmed down, has a personal trainer, and even bought his own tanning bed." He snickers.

Karen shoots me a look that I interpret to mean a possible new love interest he's trying to impress. Maybe even quite a bit younger.

"What do you think changed, if you don't mind my asking?" Karen inquires.

"I think something new is interesting him. I do not know what. I am just happy to see him with a purpose again. I am excited about this weekend, and you will be part of it." Michelle hugs Karen, who laughs out loud. Michelle assures us that her father was emphatic that no gifts are to be brought. She admits she knows little about the plans for the weekend. Guests are to arrive no later than 5:00 p.m. today and stay for the following three days.

Honoré cuts in, "He did tell me that each guest will have a character name that must be used for the whole weekend. Also, each character will be given clues and must follow what they instruct."

"Wow, this sounds very elaborate. Are all the guests from the party staying at your father's house?" Karen asks Michelle.

"*Oui*. Knowing my father, the game will be incredibly detailed. At his seventy-fifth birthday, he transformed the winery into Wonderland. It was magical." She laughs. "I played Alice."

I focus on Honoré, but he keeps his gaze straight, appearing to concentrate on driving. "Michelle's brother was Tweedledee, and I, Tweedledum." I can't read his expression. The tone was flat. Is that resentment or hurt I'm sensing?

I'm curious what Honoré's take is on all of this. I know he loves Michelle, so is he excited about the weekend, or that she's happy that her father appears better? I'd like to get a better feel for what he thinks. I trust his instincts and could use some background on the host. I'd hate to offend Michelle's father in front of our friends.

A crack of thunder causes Karen to jump. The gray skies open, and a deluge of rain begins. Since leaving Paris, the country roads have begun to narrow. Two lanes on each side down to one each. Mountains climb on the right shoulder. With only headlights to illuminate the way, the increasing curves and incline of the wet lane bring me anxiety.

A sly smile creases Honoré's lips. "Do not worry, *mon ami*. I have driven these roads many times. I am, as you say, 'a professional.'"

Karen's voice emanates from the back. "Where have I heard that before? Oh, yeah, my husband."

I look between Karen and Honoré with mock distain. "*I* have *complete* faith in your driving ability. I hope this weather doesn't ruin your father-in-law's plans. Do you know what the weather forecast for the weekend is?"

"I do," Michelle says. "It is to rain this weekend very much. The winery has some big buildings, so maybe anything planned outdoors can come in. The only worry is too much rain is bad for the grape harvest."

"I would love to hear more about the winery," Karen states.

"It had been family-owned until the last family member passed away. It was abandoned for several years after that. The vines were not being tended. My father bought it about fifteen years ago, modernized it, hired people, and turned much of his attention to winemaking."

Our headlights flash across a sign that welcomes us to Marchand. That gives me some peace of mind. I know where I am, in a general sort of way. After several miles, Honoré turns the car onto a road. Road, at this point, being a loose interpretation of the term. It's more like a path. Single car wide, semi gravel, semi grass-covered, and steep. He shifts into a lower gear. Stones ding against the sides and undercarriage of the car. After what seems like forever, the road levels off, as does my breathing. We continue on the tree-lined lane until I hear the roar of thunder. It increases in intensity as if we're driving right into it. A wooden bridge appears before us. It's a river, not thunder, making the near-deafening sound. Honoré creeps onto it. The bridge creaks as we cross. My trust that this structure is safe is tested.

"It is the river Garonne. It cuts through the land. It is very fast and dangerous," Honoré states. Looking through the window and the railings, I can't see the bottom. I'm reminded that I don't like heights. I release my breath once we're off the bridge.

"We should be there in about fifteen minutes," Michelle chirps from the back.

"It's a long way from town," Karen says.

Michelle nods. "*Oui*. The vineyard is like a mountain island. It is terraced on three sides to get the most sun. Below the vineyards, the terrain is very steep and rocky. One cannot walk down it safely. The house and winery are at the top. The view is spectacular. I hope this rain ends so you can see it."

Conversations diminish until lights appear ahead of us. The warm glow from windows signals that we are at the house, or should I say "castle." Lights in the courtyard outline a large stone building. The darkness and pouring rain obscure details. Honoré maneuvers the car near the front door. A man appears with an umbrella and escorts Karen and Michelle inside.

"Should we grab our luggage?" I ask, looking to Honoré.

"*Non*. Someone will bring it in."

The first man returns with the umbrella for me. Honoré runs to the front door as a young man jumps in and moves the car.

Once inside, the warmth wraps around us. Michelle greets a tall, thin, distinguished older gentleman in a waistcoat. "*Bonjour*, Butler."

Can't Michelle remember his name? Is he new?

Honoré leans in and whispers, "The butler's last name is Butler."

How ironic is that? I slide a sideways glance to Honoré, who grins and shrugs.

Karen mumbles to herself, "Just like Phryne." Not sure what she said, I turn to Karen, who shakes her head.

"Good evening, madame. Welcome." A strong British accent accompanies a slight head bow. "The master is in his library. He asks that you join him upon arrival. Your luggage will be in your rooms momentarily."

Michelle smiles. "*Merci*." She turns to us. "Come, I will introduce you."

The hall entrance, large enough to land a small plane, has large black-and-white floor tiles in a diamond pattern, a grand sweeping marble staircase to the left outlined with ornate black wrought iron railings, and a magnificent crystal chandelier centered in the room.

Michelle steps further into the hall and gestures to a wooden door. "This way, please."

Honoré steps aside for me and Karen to follow. I put my hand on Karen's back. She shivers. "Are you alright?" I ask.

Karen leans into me. "I hear the song 'Masquerade,' from *Phantom of the Opera,* playing in my head."

"Because . . ."

"I'm not sure. It popped in the minute I saw the harlequin pattern. I was struck with a feeling of foreboding."

"Some of us need more strings to tie those tangential thoughts together," I reply with concern.

Michelle knocks before opening the door. Upon entering, she says, "*Bonjour*, Papa."

Following her into the room, Karen pats my arm. "We'll discuss it later. Alone." She shoots me a "let it go for now" look. Something in my gut doesn't want to wait. Karen's premonitions are never without merit.

The room is subdued, even cold. Dark wooden bookcases line every spare inch of wall, floor to ceiling. Deep-brown ceiling beams create recessed squares painted mossy green. Chocolate-colored, overstuffed leather chairs flank a single window, which is covered in drapes the same shade as the ceiling. The only light comes from a single brass desk lamp casting eerie shadows on the floor. An elderly man rises from the chair behind a massive dark wooden desk and steps around it to greet us. He's about 5'8", bald, with livid green eyes and an artificial tan that registers a tinge of orange. His gray pinstriped suit is immaculately tailored. Shoes are buffed to a high shine. A crisp white shirt and deep red tie complete the outfit. Curious, but who dresses for the office in their own home?

"Papa, this is Dan and Karen Novice. This is my papa, Monsieur Bres." Michelle swells with pride.

I extend my hand. "A pleasure, sir."

He firmly grabs it. A large ring digs into my fingers. He drops my hand quickly and moves to look at Karen. "You have French blood in you. The beauty is unmistakable."

Karen turns bright red. "Thank you. Yes, my father was French but died when I was very young. Thank you for the kind invitation. Your home is magnificent."

He bows his head. "*Merci.*" Monsieur Bres turns his back to Honoré after only the slightest nod of acknowledgment. Placing his hand on his daughter's arm, he says, "I am pleased you made it, *chérie.*"

"Papa, tell me your plans for the weekend, please," Michelle begs.

He chuckles, wiggling his finger negatively at her. "*Non, not even for you, ma chérie.* You are the first of the guests to arrive. When everyone is here, I will explain."

Michelle hugs her father, bestowing a kiss on his cheek. A discreet knock on the door draws our attention. Mr. Butler enters the room. "The guests' luggage has been taken to their assigned rooms, sir."

Monsieur Bres waves him off. "If you would like to follow Butler, he will show to your rooms. Cocktails at six and dinner at seven. I have some things to finish. *Au revoir.*"

We follow Butler up the marble stairs to the second floor. The room is a warm white color. Floor-to-ceiling drapes—the same color as the walls and with large red flowers—hang in front of both windows. A large bed centered on one wall has an upholstered headboard in the same fabric as the curtains. A brass chandelier hangs above the bed.

Karen releases a deep sigh. "I love it. Yellow roses in the vase. Friendship and joy."

Once alone in our room, I turn to Karen. "Now can you explain what was going on in the hall downstairs?"

Karen sighs. "The black-and-white tiles on the floor make a harlequin pattern, but that's also the name of a character from an old Italian comedy who dresses in clothes that have a diamond pattern."

"Okay, where does *The Phantom of the Opera* come in?"

"In the musical, there is a scene at a masquerade ball. The song being sung is 'Masquerade.' The Phantom crashes the party and terrifies the guests, which led me to remember a short story by Agatha Christie called "The Affair at the Victory Ball," in which a character dressed as a harlequin attends a masquerade party and is murdered."

This unsettles me. Thoughts swirl through my brain. What does it mean? Is there danger here? Karen has my "coppy senses" tingling.

"What do you think it means?" I ask.

Karen shrugs. "I don't know. It's just a feeling that hit me. Maybe it's because our last few vacations didn't go smoothly. For now, I'm gonna try to enjoy being here."

CHAPTER 3

Karen unpacks our clothes and puts the suitcases away. I pull out my phone to check my messages, but have no reception. I check the laptop, and it's the same. I'll check with Honoré later about connecting to the house Wi-Fi. For now, I'm "unplugged" without any signal. Whether that's good or bad, I'm not sure.

Karen steps into our private bathroom with our toiletries. "I'm going to take a hot bath. We still have some time before cocktails. Please ask Michelle or Honoré how formal the dress code is this evening."

"Will do. I think they're in the room next door."

I step out into the hall and notice a Middle Eastern gentleman being escorted to the room across from ours. His brown eyes never break contact with me. He inclines his head toward me, and I reciprocate. The bedroom door closes behind him. As I reach up to knock on Michelle and Honoré's bedroom door, I hear raised voices on the other side. Rapid and loud French can be heard. I listen for a few minutes for a break in the conversation. Hearing none, I take a step back, planning a silent retreat when the door pulls open. Honoré's face of anger turns to a mask of happiness with a forced smile. "Oh . . . Dan . . . did you need something?"

Trying to regain my composure, I say, "Karen was wondering how formal the dress code is for tonight." I look past Honoré's left shoulder and make eye contact with Michelle, who appears shaken and answers with a quiver in her voice, "Cocktail dress and suits for men."

"Well, thanks. I'll let Karen know," I reply, smiling at Michelle, who has a tight grin. I face Honoré. "If *anything* is wrong, you'd let me know, right?"

His shoulders relax. "*Oui. Merci, mon ami.* We will stop at your room when it is time."

I turn toward my room when the door across from Honoré's begins to open. A tall, wiry, blond-haired man sees me, then slams the door closed. I stand for a moment and contemplate. Who are the other guests? Friends? More family? Business associates? Combination of all the above? Curiouser and curiouser.

I step into my bedroom, then knock on the bathroom door before stepping in. The smell of soap hangs in the moist, warm air. Karen is lying back in the white claw-foot tub with water near the top. "What's up?" she asks.

"Some of the other guests have arrived, but more importantly, I heard Michelle and Honoré arguing."

Sitting up, she inquires, "About what?"

"I couldn't tell. It was in French."

She shakes her head from side to side. "Something's going on. I just wish I knew what. Is it too late to back out now?" She chuckles nervously.

"I saw a couple of the other guests going into their rooms."

"Do any look like competition for my world-famous detective husband?" Karen winks.

I extend my hand to help her out of the bath, then move into the bedroom to change for the evening. I decide on a black double-breasted jacket, matching pants, a white shirt, and black tie. There's a knock on the door. I open it to Honoré and Michelle. Honoré has on a deep navy jacket and slacks, light-blue shirt, and navy-and-white striped tie. Michelle is breathtaking in a three-quarter sleeve, navy, V-neck dress that hugs her curves on top and flares from her waist to mid-calf. She's wearing heeled sandals in gold. Her hair is pulled into a French twist.

I close my mouth. "You look amazing, Michelle. Please come in."

Karen steps out of the bathroom, and my heart jumps a beat. Her dress is a black, long-sleeved turtleneck that drops from her shoulders to below her knees. She leans on me while she puts on silver high heels. Her hair falls softly around her shoulders. I breathe in her perfume and smile.

"Well, I think we make a couple of very handsome couples. Shall we?" Karen says, moving into the hall.

I close the door behind me and pause. No locks. That causes an uneasiness in me. Karen reaches her hand back for me. "Dan?"

"Coming," I reply. "Michelle, I noticed we can lock our room from the inside with a slide bolt, but there's no key to lock it when we leave."

"This is my papa's home. You and your things are safe. There is no need for a key."

We head downstairs. Mr. Butler stands at the bottom. "Everyone is to join the master in the library."

The room has a different feel. Additional floor lamps have been turned on, giving the room a warmer glow then previously. Conversations flow, and waitstaff weave between people with trays of hors d'oeuvres and flutes of something bubbly, whisking away used plates, cutlery, and glasses. We make our way to greet Monsieur Bres. Michelle kisses her father's cheeks. He waves her off and states, "Please have a glass of champagne and something to eat. Introduce yourself to some of the other guests." He turns to speak to a gentleman, maybe sixty years old, nearly bald, red-faced, and thick around the middle. It makes me think he spends much of his time giving work orders to others. Karen has positioned herself against the back wall, facing both the room and the door. I grab four glasses from a passing tray. Honoré and Michelle each take one when I offer them. Karen looks up from her first sip. "Oohh, good stuff." We nibble on various appetizers. Karen and Michelle introduce themselves to several people and engage in polite conversation, while Honoré and I stand shoulder to shoulder surveying the room. I can't help but scan the room and do a threat assessment. My eyes, again, meet those of the Middle Eastern man. Piercing, intense, and confident eyes. Short-clipped black hair with a receding hairline. Late thirties, lean and muscular, clean shaven, with a flawlessly tailored gray suit. Again, we nod acknowledgement. "Coppy senses" are up on this one.

After some time, a gong rings. Mr. Butler opens the library doors and announces dinner is served. Everyone waits for our host to lead a procession to the dining room.

I hesitate momentarily at the entrance to the dining room.

It's the length and width of a basketball court with rich brown, wide wooden plank floors. White upholstered chairs and a white tablecloth appoint the huge table centered in the room. Place settings of deep blue and white make a beautiful contrast. Thick drapes in the same colors as the china hang across each window.

Karen gasps. "Gorgeous."

Name cards are displayed at each place setting. Thirteen in all. Karen and I find ours. Michelle and Honoré are sitting further down the table on the same side. My back to the door brings some anxiety. Karen rubs my shoulders in support. She knows me. The moment we are seated, a couple enters the room. Everyone turns to see who they may be. I check our host's face. His eyes flash anger in their direction.

"Pardon, Papa," offers the man. His oval face and thin black hair make him a younger version of his father, but his mossy-green eyes waver with insecurity. He places a hand on the back of his companion, directing her to the two open seats. She's round with brown hair pulled into a bun, but some hair has escaped and appears to defy the laws of gravity. Her red dress appears to be from a time when its owner was a thin person. It wrinkles and accentuates rolls in a most unflattering sense. Her eyes never look up. Both sit at the table across from Honoré and Michelle with pressed smiles on their lips.

Waitstaff appear with the first course. Karen attempts to start a conversation with the woman to her right but is unsuccessful and stops trying. Karen leans into me. "I'm not sure if she speaks English or not."

Layers of murmured conversations occur around us.

Several courses come and go. After coffee and dessert are served, Monsieur Bres taps his knife on a glass and stands. "Your attention, please. You are all aware that this is to be a murder mystery weekend. I will now lay out the rules. First, each person will be assigned a character name. You will wear a name badge, introduce yourself, and answer only to that name until the end of the game three days from now."

Concerned that this will be a repeat of the *Alice in Wonderland* party, I try to read Honoré's expression, but he is staring at the tablecloth.

Bres continues, "Second, at various intervals throughout the weekend, your character will be given clues or directions to follow. They may be a piece of the solution, or a misdirection meant to confuse players. Third, as people are from several different countries, the spoken language will be English. I am not participating. I am the judge, and my word is final. To win the game, you must solve how the murder occurred, unmask the murderer, and have never broken character. Anyone failing to maintain their character or not adhering to the clues will be eliminated from winning the grand prize of one million euros."

Gasps of surprise erupt, and heads swivel from side to side. A quick calculation tells me it's over a million U.S. dollars. Karen grabs my arm, mouthing the word "wow."

Monsieur Bres puts up his hands to quell the voices. "Each of you has a packet in your room. The game begins tomorrow morning at breakfast. Please make your way back to your rooms at this time. Good night."

He walks slowly from the room as everyone rises from their seats. Snippets of conversations can be heard. "Give it to charity." "Pay off debts." "Provide for my family." "Have a good time." Others are in languages I can't understand.

Karen, Honoré, Michelle, and I walk to our rooms. Michelle and Karen whisper to each other at the top of the stairs before Karen and I step into our room. "What were you two talking about?" I ask.

"When they get their packet, they'll come here for us to look over the information together."

On the bed are two large, cream-colored envelopes, one addressed to Karen and the other to me. Someone came in and out of our room. I open mine with trepidation, turn it over, and spill the contents onto the bed. There's a letter explaining the rules again and a name badge. "Well, you can call me Pat."

Karen knits her eyebrows together. "Pat?"

"Pat U. Downe, spelt with an 'e' at the end." Karen's attempt to repress her laugh is not successful. "Okay, if that's so funny, let's hear your name for the weekend."

"I'm Charity . . . Charity Case. I'm thinking he has an off-center sense of humor, or he regards social workers about as well as he does detectives," Karen replies, shaking her head. A knock at the door draws our attention. "Come in," Karen says, louder than needed.

Honoré and Michelle step in, each holding their envelope. He's also carrying a bottle. Honoré puts his hand out for me to shake. "I'm Marshall Law. Pleased to meet you." His tone sounds lighthearted, but it isn't reflected in his eyes.

All heads turn to Michelle, who grins. "I'm Olive Yew. I guess Papa loves me most." Karen and I reveal our *nom de plumes*.

Honoré raises the bottle. "Cognac, *mon ami*. I think we will need much alcohol before the weekend is over."

I grab water glasses off the dresser when there's a second knock on our door. Michelle opens it, and the two late arrivals at dinner step into the room. Michelle hugs both, then turns to us. "I would like to introduce my brother Jules and his wife, Camille."

Karen and I shake both their hands. Honoré nods to them.

"It's so nice to meet you both," Karen says with a smile. "Do you work with your father?"

"*For* my father!" he replies. "I am the chief accountant. My wife has a store in the village that sells items from local farmers and artists."

Karen leans forward. "I would love to see that. It's nice to shop local and find unique gifts. I wonder if we could see it this weekend?"

"I think my father-in-law has the weekend scheduled, but when you go back to Paris, I will open my store for you to look in private," states Camille.

"That's very kind of you. Thank you," Karen replies.

"What are your names for the weekend?" Michelle asks her brother.

His jaw clenches. "I am Justin . . . Sane. My wife is Joy Kil. I see you are still the favorite, Sister. Do I call you Olive or Ms. Yew?"

Apparently Honoré isn't the only family member to be bothered by the disrespect from Monsieur Bres. Michelle gives her brother a disapproving look.

"Michelle, a million euros? Can your dad afford it, and why such a huge prize?" I ask.

"*Oui*, my father is worth over one hundred million euros. I think he is ready to retire and start to enjoy all he has earned. He has an eight-week cruise booked for next month and a two-month chalet rental in Switzerland at Christmas."

"I can't even imagine what that kind of money looks like," I mumble more to myself than to anyone else.

Michelle laughs out loud. "That is my papa. He is kind and generous. I do not think that anyone will win that big prize, but he will make sure all his guests have a fun weekend and leave with a nice gift."

Honoré's eyes are focused on the carpet, his face an unreadable mask. What's that about? Tensions with having a rich father-in-law, who I can't believe is as kind as Michelle portrays, or maybe he doesn't want to play "the game"? I'll approach him about it later when we're alone. Jules' tight jaw twitches.

"Did someone say 'helicopter'?" My attention focuses back on the conversation.

"*Oui*, my father just bought one for himself. He has always wanted to learn to fly. Now he is looking for a pilot to teach him." Michelle snickers. "I am happy he has made plans for more play and less work."

"He doesn't own one for business?" I question.

Jules nods. "He does, but it is bigger and for more people. He wants one for himself."

My interest piqued, I ask, "Is it here?"

"It was delivered yesterday. Some old buildings needed to be torn down. The open space was made into a landing pad," Michelle states.

Before I can respond, Karen jumps in, "You're speaking to Dan's heart. He's always wanted to learn how to fly a helicopter. I'm sure he and Honoré will need to run over and look at it, if these storms let up."

Michelle hugs Karen. "I am so glad you are here. Maybe we can have a bet?" She slides a sideways glance at Karen and Camille. "Female detectives against male detectives."

Karen's head pops up. "Oh, like teams. Us against them." Karen points her index finger at Honoré, Jules, and me. "Sure, if that's allowed." We each read over the rules, and it is not forbidden to have teams.

I elbow Honoré. "I believe the gauntlet has been thrown down. We accept your challenge."

He utters "*Oui*" through a forced smile. Jules declines the offer for both him and Camille, remarking that as the heir, it could appear a conflict of interest. They are part of the game, but not actively trying to win.

"I will play, and if I win, my money will go to charity," Michelle states.

"Do either of you know any of the other guests?" I search the faces of Michelle and Honoré.

"*Non*," Michelle sighs. Jules shakes his head negatively.

Honoré begins to pour cognac for each of us.

Jules waves him off. "Camille and I are tired. We are going to bed." He nods in our direction. "It was nice to meet you. We will see you at breakfast." Both head out into the hall.

Karen and I sit on the bed while Honoré and Michelle sit in the two chairs in the room.

"Until tomorrow. For now, a drink among good friends."

Karen raises her glass. We tap ours together. "*Santé*," we say in unison. Conversation shifts to detective skills that may be needed, who might be competition, and speculating on what we'd spend the money on if we win. Laughter helps to visibly ease the tension in Honoré. His shoulders relax, and his true smile returns. Time slips away until we need to turn in.

CHAPTER 4

A crack of thunder wakes me. Karen's sleep is undisturbed. A glance at the clock doesn't make sense. It reads 6:30 a.m., but the room is far too dark for this time of the morning. I slide stealthily out of bed. The drapes are open; however, there's little natural light. Torrents of rain break over the house. A fleeting thought occurs to me: does Monsieur Bres have enough money to order this weather as a setting detail for his murder mystery weekend? I snort a laugh in response to my own question.

I head to the bathroom. Showered and dressed, I decide on a self-guided tour. Lights illuminate the hall as I step into it. I wander down the stairs and see a soft glow from the dining room. When I enter, Mr. Butler is setting out coffee cups on the table.

He stands up straight when he notices me. "Sir, coffee will be ready momentarily. Breakfast is at 8:00."

"Thank you. I'll let you get back to it. Excuse me," I say, stepping out of the room. Once back in the hall, I orient myself. There is a narrow hall that runs past the library and under the staircase. I start down it when a young woman in a traditional black-and-white maid's uniform, holding a carafe, pops out of what I guess is the kitchen and scurries toward the dining room. She nods. "*Bonjour.*" The smell of warm bread, cooked meat, and coffee trail behind her. Momentarily considering backtracking to its source, I abandon the idea when I notice a set of double doors on the other side of the hall from the dining room. After a quick glance around the room, I sneak over and open them. A few feet in, then I wait for my eyes to adjust. Two sides have floor-to-ceiling windows but offer limited light. It's the formal living room. The walls and ceiling seem to be painted white with three evenly spaced gold and crystal chandeliers. A huge marble fireplace is centered on the interior wall. There are three separate sitting areas, one in front of the fireplace, another offset from the door, and then one further in the room. The furniture is shades of white and soft blues. I back out, pulling the doors closed as I do until I bump into someone. I spin on my heels to find myself face-to-face with Honoré. "You scared the liver out of me. You're like a cat," I say.

He grins at me. "You were like a cat burglar. What were you doing in there?"

I shrug. "Just bein' nosy. Hey, I think the coffee's ready. Let's grab a cup."

He laughs heartily, slaps me on the back, and heads to the dining room. I'm two steps behind him. Once we each have a cup, I hesitantly approach him. "Is something else going on here that I should know about?"

"Come with me while I have a cigarette," he says dryly, standing up with his coffee in hand.

My head snaps up. "I didn't know you smoked."

"Because I do not" is his reply while he walks toward the hall.

"Aah!" I pick up my cup and follow him. He runs outside through the pouring rain, crosses the driveway, and goes into the garage. He gets into the driver's side of his car, and I sit in the passenger's.

Honoré turns a serious face to me. "I swear the house has listening devices. This is between you and me. I love my wife, and she loves her father. I would never do anything to hurt her, but I do not want to 'play this game.'" He uses finger air quotes.

"I understand doing things we don't like for the love of a wife." I let loose a low chuckle. "But I heard the anger in your voice the night we arrived."

He slowly nods. "You may have noticed the lack of respect my father-in-law has for me. I have had forty years of it. The older I get, the less I tolerate it. I was tired, hungry, and got angry. I am sorry you had to hear it."

"Yeah, I noticed he's not your biggest fan. What does Michelle say about it?"

Honoré drops his head back against the headrest. "She is the most positive person I know. She wants me and her father to be friends. I do not know when she thinks that will happen."

I snicker, as does he. "Okay, we're a team. Let's enjoy what we can this weekend. It's only three days," I say, stretching my hand toward him.

He grasps it tightly. "*Oui*." He reaches for the door handle before facing me. "One more thing, *mon ami*. We have married smart and, I think, somewhat dangerous women. They could very well win this weekend."

I step out of the car. "You don't have to tell me." We sigh in unison and make a run for the house. The rain has not abated one bit.

We reach the inside of the hall and shake off like well-mannered dogs. Our wives are standing at the bottom of the staircase with their hands on their hips, looking at us. "What?" we ask.

Karen guffaws and shakes her head as she and Michelle walk toward the dining room. Honoré and I look at each and shrug. We join Karen and Michelle for breakfast. Both are wearing their name tags. Karen hands mine to me, and Michelle holds out Honoré's.

A magnificent breakfast buffet has been laid out: egg casserole, sausages and bacon, fresh fruit, yogurt, a variety of cheeses, warm croissants, and baguettes, along with beverages. Many of the guests from the night before are present. Our host is absent. Others wander in one at a time. All are wearing the required name badges.

Jules and Camille join our table, then we move to the buffet line. I find myself behind the mysterious Middle Eastern man. He turns to look at me.

"Hi, I'm Pat U. Downe," I say.

He puts his hand out for me to shake. "I'm Dr. Hurt. Dr. I. M. Hurt," he replies with a Middle Eastern accent. We shake hands.

"So, what form of medicine do you practice, Doctor?" I ask.

"For this weekend, I hope none." He laughs out loud. "I heard that there were to be two police officers this weekend. I guess you are the second after Oliver's son-in-law."

I bow my head.

There's a tap on my shoulder from behind. I swivel my head and find the bald, red-faced man I saw during cocktails the night we arrived. His plate is piled with several portions of every dish. "I'm Bill. Bill Ding. Get it? Can you guess what I do?" he asks in an annoyingly nasal British accent while he plops two croissants on top of his plate and licks the fingers of his right hand, which he places out in front of him. I choose to give him a fist bump and reply, "Construction."

"Close. I own a construction firm that has built a *huge* number of buildings around the world. I've built plenty for Oliver." He jerks his head as if indicating our host is in the room.

"Good to know you," I answer.

Karen, Michelle, and Honoré are seated when I arrive at the table. "I met two of the guests," I say, then summarize what they each told me.

Jules and Camille sit down. Karen reports, "I met the curly-haired, blond man. He's a restaurant reviewer from Germany. His name is Corey . . . Ander. He's the guy sitting alone." Karen lowers her voice. "He's a bit eccentric. He looked at the bowl of dry-roasted peanuts like they bite. I wasn't sure what was wrong. He said he has recently developed a severe nut allergy. How do ya eat out all the time with that?" We all shake our heads.

The gong is struck, and Mr. Butler clears his throat. "Ladies and gentlemen, your attention, please. Your first challenge is to meet all the other guests before leaving this room. You may be called upon to collaborate with or conspire against them. Thank you."

Karen moves to talk to a middle-aged woman with short-clipped, gray hair. I sit down with one of the other people I haven't met. "Hi, I'm Pat U. Downe."

He brings his face up from his plate. Steel black eyes with no readily visible pupils cause me to draw back. Thick, salt-and-pepper curls flop in rhythm while he chews and slurps his drink. My investigator's nose hits on either that's not coffee or it's not solely coffee. Another whiff floods me with memories of arresting drunks, that slightly sour smell of alcohol and body odor.

"*Sì, es* nice to meet you. You are a policeman, *sì*? Well, I am Fire Chief . . ." He turns his badge over and looks at it. ". . . Les Burn. It is another bad firefighter joke." His Italian accent is unmistakable. He smirks and returns to eating.

"Nice to meet you. Good luck this weekend," I say. He gives me a thumbs-up and takes another slurp.

I hurry back to the table with Karen and the others. She's half-whispering to Michelle, "The other woman is Estelle Hertz. She works as a surgical nurse for the doctor at his practice in Canada. She's from there."

"That's nice the doctor brought her with," I say.

"He didn't. She received her own separate invitation," Karen states.

Michelle looks around. "Hon . . . Marshall and I met Duane Pipe. He's a plumber from South Africa. He looks familiar to me, but I can't remember from where. It will come to me." Karen and Michelle are busy making notes on each person.

Karen looks up. "Between us, we've met everyone that was at dinner last night. Twelve guests and then your father as host."

Twelve guests. Same as on a jury, and Monsieur Bres announced he's the judge. I'd say it's coincidence, but I don't believe in them as a rule. So, why then?

We're finishing our breakfast when Mr. Butler announces that everyone is free to wander the buildings and the grounds at our leisure but should be aware that clues will be delivered later today. Sandwiches and salads will be laid out at noon. Dinner will be served at 8:00 p.m. The gong will ring at 7:30 to remind everyone.

Jules and Camille excuse themselves and head to their room. Karen suggests she and Michelle go to our room to make a suspect board. Michelle says that she'll stop in her father's office for supplies.

I stand up and look at Michelle. "How will we know who the 'victim' is? Will it be a guest or another person we haven't met?"

Michelle knits her eyebrows together. "I do not know that. I think we get that information today."

A look of concern sweeps across Karen's face. "What's wrong?" I ask.

"Nothing. Just thinking." She pats my arm reassuringly and smiles. My "coppy senses" tingle otherwise. I dismiss probing further . . . for now.

Once in the hall, I notice the lights in the living room and motion for Honoré to join me. The room glows with soft colors. A fire in the fireplace beckons us to sit. We lose track of time talking about old cases and friends lost when Karen and Michelle join us. They're eager to tell us about their color-coded system for suspects, clues, weapons, motives, and opportunity. Michelle even found an old bulletin board to pin everything to.

"You're very serious about this game," I say.

"Yeah, we are! Mich . . . I mean, Olive and I talked about the charities we're supporting, if we win. We're excited and want to enjoy this as much as possible," Karen states.

"But now, I want to show you my father's winery. There is a tunnel to take us there without getting wet." Once there, Michelle happily explains the various rooms associated with the winery.

We meet the master winemaker, Louis, who explains the process from grapes to wine. Honoré notices the time on his watch, and we make our way back for lunch. After lunch, we return to our rooms.

Two pink envelopes are on the bed. Karen opens the one addressed to her. "Oh, it's our first clue. We need to verbalize them at dinner, but I'll tell you mine now. I used to date Dr. I. M. Hurt but broke up with him because my family didn't approve. I'm now dating you, Pat, because you need a strong mother figure and I want to 'save you,'" she says, pointing to me. "But I'm still interested in the doctor." She grins.

I read mine aloud. "Okay, I'm second-in-command after Marshall Law, but I want to be chief. I'm also suing Duane Pipe for a poor plumbing job that caused damage to my house."

"So, I wonder if I'm the murderer, because I sound like a basket full of hang-ups," Karen says, rolling her eyes.

"I hope I don't kill Hon . . . Marshall to get ahead."

Karen and I head to Michelle and Honoré's room to compare clues. I knock on the door. Honoré answers, and we find Jules and Camille already there. We sit on the bed.

Honoré sighs. "I'm the police chief, but I want to be a high court judge and need Justin's endorsement."

Michelle pats Karen's arm. "Dear, I am a beauty consultant and feel you need a major makeover, but I am being charged with fraud. I have been repacking another manufacturer's product as mine, and Bill Ding reported me to the press. He is ruining my business."

"I am a vegan and believe all animal life is precious. Corey Ander reported a drop in patrons because of the protests I have been leading outside of his restaurants," Camille comments softly. We all turn our eyes to Jules.

"I am mayor and have blocked Bill Ding's new project because I am interested in Estelle Hertz and she wants to start a clinic where the project is proposed to be."

Karen nudges Michelle, who has been taking notes on each person, their motivations, and possible victims.

Michelle looks up. "I will take notes at dinner and add them to our board. I hope we learn who the victim is." We agree to meet after the first gong and head into dinner together.

CHAPTER 5

The gong rings. Dress for the evening is more relaxed. Karen wears a black crepe pantsuit, and I put on dress pants and French cuff dress shirt. We step into the hall, join Honoré, Michelle, Jules, and Camille, and move to the dining room. The room is buzzing with conversations and laughter as we enter.

Mr. Butler hands each of us a card with numbers on it. "As you can see, there are three smaller tables, each numbered. There will be three courses, including a pairing of alcohol. You will be required to switch tables with each course. A bell will signal the end of the course. Please move to the corresponding table in the exact order as it appears on your card. You are to interact with the characters that join you. Learn what you can. Beware of whom you dine with, be they a victim or murderer."

I notice Monsieur Bres occupies a single table at the front of the room.

Karen winks at Michelle. "Let the competition begin. I start at Table 2." We each note our tables and move to them. Karen gives me a quick peck on the cheek.

I sit at Table 1 and am joined by Michelle/Olive Yew, Dr. I. M. Hurt, and Les Burn, the fire chief. The first course is served: a salad with mixed greens, tart apple pieces, and an apple vinaigrette, along with flutes of champagne. I bite into the first piece and enjoy the flavor when Les looks at Michelle. "Olive, I know you are not an honest businesswoman, but I cannot prove it."

Michelle's character looks offended. "That is not true. I believe in my product. My night cream can give your skin a youthful glow. Maybe you should try it."

Dr. Hurt snaps, "Do not start on her. I intend to marry her. I would never be involved with anyone who is not honest." He pats Michelle's hand.

She smiles at him. "Thank you, dearest."

Les switches his gaze to me. "How is your son . . . the arsonist? You will have a hard time becoming chief of police if people find that out." He snickers and raises his glass to me. He empties it in one gulp and signals Mr. Butler for a refill.

I drop my fork. "I can't believe that of my son. I don't think you can prove he did anything."

"Maybe we should talk about what I can or can't prove in private and see how much it is worth to you," Les says while finishing his second glass of champagne. He requests a third.

The banter continues through the course until the bell rings.

At Table 2, I find Jules/Justin Sane, Bill Ding, the engineer, and Duane Pipe, the plumber. Mr. Butler provides a round of French 75. Smooth and cool, it goes down without any effort.

"I really need you to allow the building permit, Mayor Sane," Bill announces.

"Well, that won't happen as Estelle Hertz wants to open a free clinic. I would not help anyone who self-promoted on a reality show," Justin retorts.

Bill turns to Duane with a mocking tone. "Well, at least I won, unlike Duane here who came in second. Too bad for him."

"I should have won! I'm the better man," Duane snaps back.

I jump in. "Wait, you're not better. Your poor plumbing job caused major damage in my house. You still refuse to make it right."

"'Cause the damage was not the fault of my company. Report to your insurance company and be quiet." Duane flicks his hand at me dismissively. He signals for another round of drinks.

Conversation slows as we tuck into the main course. Braised short ribs with a red wine reduction, potato puree, and glazed baby carrots. I may have hummed out loud with each mouthful. I realize I need to sip my drinks as a buzz is beginning to start. We speculate on the game, who will be a victim and who is the murderer.

Duane looks from side to side as if about to share a secret. We all lean in. "I have to say, the food has been amazing so far," Duane states and leans back. All heads nod in unison.

I clean my plate. I miss eating with Karen, mainly because I love her company and she doesn't finish everything, so I get seconds.

Bill snaps his head in Honoré/Marshall's direction. "I hope I get to talk to him. We need to discuss the small matter of a ticket I need to get out of."

The bell rings. I make my way to Table 3. Estelle Hertz, the nurse, Corey Ander, the chef and restaurant critic, and Camille/Joy Kil are seated, as are glasses of Moscato.

"I understand that you know Olive Yew. I think her products are the best," Estelle gushes.

Corey smirks. "Well, most women need some improvement. Good thing there's something to help. I know most of the ladies here are interested in me, even you." He sneers in Camille's direction. "You can stop protesting outside of my restaurants. It will not stop us from serving what customers want: meat!"

Camille puts the back of her hand to her forehead. "Oh, the poor animal souls . . . it's cruel to eat them. I will not stop."

"I'm not interested in you," Estelle says. "You're opinionated, overweight, and hurtful to people. Mayor Justin Sane is a great man. I think the world of him."

"You're interested in Justin?" I ask.

Estelle grins. "He's stopping that terrible building that Bill Ding wants to put up. I petitioned the mayor, and he believes in me."

Dessert arrives. A caramel crunch cake, warm milk chocolate drizzled over the top, and a scoop of salted caramel ice cream. If a murder does take place, it would happen if someone tried to take this away from Karen. I'm about to put a spoonful in my mouth when shouting from across the room stops me. Everyone's head swivels to see what it's about.

Les Burn has jumped up so fast he knocks his chair over. He's leaning on the table, yelling, "Why did you say that? It is not true. You cannot say that about me. Why did you say it? WHY?"

Duane Pipe is looking around, completely flushed, and stammers, "That . . . that was my clue to reveal. It was in my room last night. I am sorry. I did not mean to upset you." He casts a glance at Monsieur Bres, who is sitting at his table with a placid expression.

Les turns toward Monsieur Bres. "Someone will pay for this lie. I will not play this stupid game." He grabs a bottle of liquor from Mr. Butler's hands and staggers from the room with the guests gawking. Murmurs erupt in the room. Karen comes to my side.

"Did you hear what the clue was that set Les off?" I ask.

"We'll discuss it in private," she replies with a "not now" look. I turn toward where Monsieur Bres had been sitting, but he's gone. Where could he have gone that fast? I would've noticed him leaving. Honoré and Michelle join us.

"I think the party's over," I mutter to myself. "Did you see your father leave?" I question Michelle.

Michelle looks over both shoulders. "I was not watching. This was upsetting. It is late. I am sure he went to bed. I feel bad this happened on his birthday weekend."

We make our way upstairs. I want to speak with Karen alone. I place my hand on her back and steer her toward our room without offering Honoré or Michelle an invitation to join us.

Once inside the room, Karen turns to me. "What's up?"

Remembering Honoré's conviction that the building has listening devices, I offer, "I'd like to run a hot bath for you." I place my finger to my lips and point to my ears to signal someone listening.

Karen nods in acknowledgement. "That's very sweet of you." We step into the bathroom and turn on the water in the bathtub and the sink.

"What was said that set Les Burn off?" I inquire.

"I can't remember exactly, but Duane Pipe said something like, 'Your arson reports aren't always accurate, especially when there's an insurance payout waiting.' That's when Les Burn jumped up and started demanding why that was said. I felt so bad for Duane."

I wonder why *that* clue set him off. Was it just a mistake, or was it a serious betrayal of a secret? My "coppy senses" are tingling. This mystery party feels like it's taken a darker turn. Is Les Burn the intended victim or the murderer?

Karen turns the water off and heads into the bedroom. I hear her scream, "Whoa!"

I race out of the bathroom. "What?"

She laughs. "Sorry. I moved my pillow, and something fell over. Scared the heck out of me. But it's just a small box of truffles. That's really kind." She shows the inside of the box to me.

I lift my pillow and have one too.

"I'm so full. I'll just nibble one now and the rest in the morning," she announces as she bites into one of the chocolates.

"Morning?"

"There are two caramel and now one chocolate. With coffee it could be a nice way to start my day."

I shake my head. My wife's love of anything sugar, anytime, still amazes me. Karen changes and slips into bed.

My mind is racing. I decide to walk around downstairs, maybe find a book to read. I step into the hallway and notice Mr. Butler, holding a cup, knocking on Corey Ander's door without an answer.

"Is everything okay?" I call out.

"Mr. Ander requested a cup of hot chocolate be brought up to him, but now he doesn't answer" is his reply.

"He could have fallen asleep or stepped into the bathroom. Try the door."

Mr. Butler turns the knob, then slowly opens the door, calling out, "Hello, Mr. Anders." No answer. No sound of any kind. I move past Butler, push the door open further, and call out again. I step around the bed. That's when I notice him. He's on the floor, in his robe, eyes open, tongue out, mouth dripping froth. I feel for a pulse. Nothing. "Get the doctor," I snap. Mr. Butler puts the cup on the dresser and hurries out. Voices and movement can be heard in the hall. I look up to see the doctor and Honoré in the doorway. I scan the room. Clothes and personal items are thrown about. Was someone looking for something? Was *he* looking for something?

Dr. Hurt bumps the truffle box as it sits on the floor, picks it up, and places it on the bed. He turns Corey over. Using his stethoscope, he places it on Corey's chest. He looks up and shakes his head negatively.

"What do you think?" I ask Dr. Hurt.

"My first thought was heart attack, but he has hives and his tongue and lips are swollen. I think it is anaphylactic shock causing the heart attack. He should have an EpiPen if he has severe allergies." One sits in full view on the nightstand.

"If he had an attack, would he have had time to get to his EpiPen, and if yes, then why did he not?" Honoré questions.

Dr. Hurt responds, "Yes. Normally the first symptoms are

itching, throat tightening, shortness of breath. That is why sufferers keep a rescue pen close to them. It appears to be a tragic situation. I would list cause of death as 'accidental.'"

"Thank you, Doctor. We need to seal the room until the authorities arrive," I say, motioning for him to step out into the hall.

"I will go for my father-in-law and notify him of what has happened. I'll meet you in the study," Honoré says.

Once in the hall, Mr. Butler closes the door. I head to the study to use the phone when I realize I don't speak French and have no authority here. But I can't resist picking up the receiver . . . nothing. I press several buttons, and still nothing. Honoré and Monsieur Bres appear.

"There's no dial tone. Do I need to do something special?" I say, looking between them.

Monsieur Bres shakes his head. "No, the phones do not work when we have terrible storms. The internet does not either. I needed to speak with a business associate but was unable to. Tomorrow morning, I will send one of the staff into the village for the gendarmerie." I have no clue what that is, and my face must reveal that.

Honoré leans over to me. "Gendarmeries are the police in smaller French villages."

"So, we're cut off from the outside at this moment. Why not send someone tonight?" I inquire skeptically.

"No," snaps Monsieur Bres. "The road that leads from here is dangerous, especially at night and with the rain."

Not wanting to be rude to my host, having no jurisdiction, and technically being on vacation, I repress my protest. My mind races over what evidence could be lost after hours. Monsieur Bres leads us out of the study.

We climb the stairs and head to our rooms. Monsieur Bres says good night and leaves us. I grab Honoré's arm. "Are we really gonna wait until morning for the police?"

"What do you think, *mon ami*? I have no authority to investigate here, and you . . . well, you have even less." He laughs, patting me on the back. "You heard the doctor. It is just a terrible accident. Nothing to worry about. Let us go to bed, see our wives, and in the morning let the locals do the work." He turns on his heels.

Karen is sitting up when I come in. "Where have you been?"

I recap what's happened and my feelings that something seems off. Karen shoots me a sideways glance. "Oh, that's horrible. I feel so bad for him. The morning will bring the right people to do the job, so just please, leave it. Dan, please don't investigate."

"Yeah, you're right . . . you're right." I flop back onto the bed and stare at the ceiling, replaying the scene. I get up to finish what I had started before: finding a book written in English from the study. I'm successful. My plan is to read until I finally fall asleep. My foot touches the top of the landing, and my eyes see Corey Ander's door. I convince myself to go inside and photograph the scene on my phone without anyone knowing. I'm taking one of the last pictures when "Daniel!" echoes in the room. I spin around. Karen's standing in the doorway, glaring at me.

I press my finger to my lips. She sighs and rolls her eyes.

I snap a couple of final shots and back out, closing the door behind me. No one will know it was me. I grab Karen's arm, and we hurry back to our room.

"You have serious short-term memory loss," Karen states, arms crossed on her chest.

"Huh?"

"I asked you to *not* investigate this. What do I find you doing? Investigating. Not our problem."

"I hear what you're saying, but something's off. I figured I'd take a couple of pictures, then look them over in private. Maybe you'd like to help?" I snuggle up to Karen, rubbing her shoulder with my shoulder.

"Ugh . . . fine," she agrees. I slide through the pictures one by one.

"Why is everything on the floor? Were you and Honoré searching for something?" Karen asks.

"No, it was that way when the door was opened."

"A terrible fate for those fabulous truffles. I guess it's too late for the thirty-second rule." Karen squints and grabs the phone, pulling it close to her face. "Are those black roses in the vase?"

"Yeah. Kinda ugly."

Deep concern sweeps across Karen's face. "That can't be a coincidence. They symbolize death. You may be right about this situation being more than an accident."

CHAPTER 6

A fretful night leads to another gray, raining day. My intention is that Honoré and I head into town for the local police when done with breakfast. A quick shower, then I throw clothes on and depart to the dining room for coffee and to meet up with Honoré.

Honoré strolls into the room. "*Bonjour, mon ami.* Are you ready for round two of this murder mystery weekend?"

My mouth hangs open for a moment. "Are you ready for the local police? We have a dead guy upstairs. Have you forgotten?"

Honoré closes his eyes momentarily, then opens them to laser-focus on me. "I have *not* forgotten. They will come and see it for what it is, a terrible accident. Nothing else. Stop making it more."

We're not on the same page here. I try a new tact. "You're right. How about you and I drive into town, contact the police, and explain the situation, professionals to professionals?"

"No need. My father-in-law will send a staff member. We players cannot leave, or we forfeit the prize. We can talk to the police when they are here." Honoré pours a cup of coffee.

Mr. Butler addresses us both. "I am sorry, sirs, but it

appears breakfast will be delayed as the additional servers from town that were hired for the weekend have not arrived yet this morning, weather being what it is." He bows out of the room. The weather is bad, but people should be able to make it up and down the drive. What's going on? Why wouldn't the staff come to work?

"Honoré, can you think of a reason they didn't show up?"

He shakes his head negatively.

I bump elbows with him. "I bet we could investigate. It may be simply a car broken down or they're having difficulty getting up here. Road trip." I cock my head to one side like an eager dog.

"Be patient. The weather will improve. We will call the police. One day will not make a difference."

"Fine," I spit out. "I'll go alone. One day can matter! I want to see for myself why the other staff haven't arrived. Where are the keys?" I firmly plant my legs and set my jaw.

Honoré looks at me and I at him. "I will get my car keys, and we will drive into town, *oui*?"

"Brilliant idea." I wink at him. We head to the hall for rain gear. Outside, sheets of rain cover us.

I look straight up. "Really? Enough already," I say. The response is a giant drop of water in my eye. No respect.

Once in the car, the wipers are on, and lights illuminate little ahead of us. Honoré maneuvers the car down the road, slowly. The angle of descent appears steeper than when we arrived. The tires in back slip out, and the car pitches sideways. After what feels like inching our way down, we arrive where the entrance to the bridge should be. Headlights reveal that a knee-deep mudslide has covered the road and torn away one of the side rails. I see Honoré drumming his fingers on the steering wheel; however, the roar of the river below drowns out all other sound. This explains why the other staff members haven't arrived from town, which means neither will the police. We are completely cut off.

Honoré carefully turns the car around and creeps his way back up to the house, mostly on an angle, until we're back in the garage. "I will make my father-in-law aware of the bridge and road situation. We will need to process the room to preserve the scene. Do you have an evidence kit with you?"

I snap, "You understand that I'm on vacation, right?"

He guffaws. "So, 'no' to having an evidence kit. I have a few things in my trunk. Let me get them. We will need to check for a place to store the body."

"You have evidence collection gear in your car? Why?"

He cocks his head to one side and exhales. "Because *I* am still working and I'm in a small village without technicians. Sometimes I have to do all the work."

I nod in appreciation of that. I found myself doing the same thing in my career.

The kit is black and the size of a large fishing tackle box. Kit retrieved, we run for the front hall through the continued downpour. Once inside, we pull off our rain gear. Honoré goes to find Monsieur Bres. I head upstairs to talk to Karen. She's dressed, coming down the stairs. "You're back. Are the police with you?" She cranes her neck back and forth to look around me.

Hesitantly, I say, "No. There's a problem."

After I summarize what I know, she replies, "So, we're trapped . . . with a dead body . . . for who knows how long. Is that what you're saying?"

"Yup."

"That poor man has been lying dead on the floor of his room for hours, and you and Honoré are now the investigating officers?"

"Got it in one," I quip.

I may have overstepped as she starts to rub her temples with her fingertips, muttering, "Why do I bother to go on vacation with you? Why?" As it's a rhetorical question, I don't reply.

She holds up both of her hands and sighs. "Okay, you and Honoré do what you have to do. I'm going down to breakfast. I'll meet with Michelle to see if we need a plan to help out during the weekend. We'll meet later." She continues down the stairs, shaking her head the whole time.

The door to Corey Ander's room isn't locked. I open it and step into the room. Low light causes me to pause and wait for my eyes to adjust. I slowly advance through the room, making a mental inventory. Honoré joins me and asks me to photograph with his phone. He's wearing gloves and hands me a pair. He dusts for fingerprints throughout. I finish with the photos. Honoré hands me bags to search for and collect items such as hair, fibers, and personal belongings, including the victim's cell phone. Hopefully his next of kin can be located on it. Each item is also photographed before being bagged and tagged appropriately. I take the deceased's prints for elimination. The victim's passport is tucked in the pocket of his suitcase. It's issued from Germany. His real name is Drew Taylor. It gives me pause when scenes are personalized.

Honoré turns to me. "Why are you bagging those things? His deodorant, his medications, including the EpiPen, and the truffles from the floor?"

"I want to be sure that anything that might be suspect is preserved. If this is an accident, fine, but I want things in custody that can be tested and, in my opinion, should be. There's something wrong here. I feel it."

"The doctor listed cause of death as accidental."

"He's not a pathologist. I believe he's coming to a conclusion based on what he's been told, not diagnostics."

Honoré nods his head in agreement but says nothing more.

A cough from the doorway catches my attention. Mr. Butler is there with a large rolling cart. "Beg your pardon, gentlemen. When you are through, we can move Mr. Ander to a refrigerator in the winery."

Honoré and I scan the room one more time. The three of us lift the body, cover it with a sheet, and push the cart to the back of the mansion. At the end of the hallway, Mr. Butler presses a button. An elevator, paneled to blend with the wall, opens, and we move the cart in. We debark in the basement, moving through the underground tunnel to the winery that has a large walk-in refrigerator. We leave the body on the cart and secure the closed door with a large padlock. Honoré places the key in his pocket.

He instructs Mr. Butler to have the guests and any additional staff join us in the dining room. Honoré has a list of everyone currently on the premises. Mr. Butler bows and heads back to the main house. Honoré and I check the door once more. Confident it's locked, we make our way to the dining room.

Once everyone is assembled, Honoré explains the situation. Gasps erupt as well as multiple questions. He patiently answers each one, sometimes repeatedly. He explains that each person will be asked to provide fingerprints, hair, and saliva swabs, all for elimination purposes.

Bill Dings verbally objects. "What I understand is this is a terrible accident, not murder. That is what I heard the doctor say. I am not giving you all that. There is no need." All eyes turn to Dr. Hurt, who explains that it does appear to be little more than a tragic accident. Honoré again explains that we are gathering as much as we can for when the officials arrive. Several others voice similar complaints. Some nod in agreement.

"At that time and with the proper authority, I'll do it. Not before." Bill Ding walks out of the room. He's followed by Duane Pipe and Les Burn.

Monsieur Bres speaks rapidly in French. He and his staff submit to everything, as do Honoré, Michelle, Jules, Camille, Karen, Dr. Hurt, Estelle Hertz, and I. We take samples and label each one. Dr. Hurt and Ms. Hertz each return to their room.

Michelle starts, "My father has many supplies, so we have sufficient food. The chef, head maid, butler, and winery manager are live-in. All the others are day help only. So, we will need to make up our own food plates from the kitchen and return them after each meal. Also, we must be responsible to maintain our rooms and the common areas of the house." She searches Karen's face, then mine. Her eyes hold so much sadness. "I am sorry, my friends. This is not the fun time I hoped for."

Karen pats her hand. "It's fine. Just one more 'aventure' for us." I snicker under my breath. That was what our son, Eric, called a new and different experience when he was a child. Karen and I have adopted it for unexpected situations.

Jules breaks in, "I spoke to my father, and the murder mystery game will continue. He feels we need a diversion as we cannot leave. Round Two will begin at dinner. Each player will receive a second clue."

I'm surprised that the game is ongoing versus leaving the guests to occupy themselves as they choose.

CHAPTER 7

Once we're back upstairs in our bedroom, Karen sits on the bed, muttering to herself and shaking her head.

"What're ya thinkin'?" I ask.

"I'm not sure. This weekend feels contrived and darker than it should be. We were never given the name of a victim, but now someone is dead. Corey Ander was terrified of accidentally eating nuts, yet he ate a truffle from an unknown source. Even if he did try one, he'd be sure his EpiPen was near him. You said it looked as if he didn't get to it in time. Well, why not?"

I shrug in response.

She continues, "The butler's name is Mr. Butler. Really?" Karen looks at me as if I have an answer.

"To play the devil's advocate, it's a murder mystery weekend. We all have our *nom de plumes*. Mr. Butler could be playing a part too."

"I don't think so. When we arrived, Michelle greeted him as 'Mr. Butler.' How would she have known that if he was another character for this weekend?"

Karen has my thoughts racing. Is there something more to Corey Ander's death, but why? And more importantly . . . who?

"Mr. Butler is the name of the butler in the *Miss Fisher's Murder Mysteries* books by Kerry Greenwood. That's too coincidental."

"Monsieur Bres may have been planning this for a while. He said the prize was a million euros. He'd want the winner to really earn it or work toward everyone failing. Mr. Butler could be more than just a butler. He could be a saboteur."

She lets out a prolonged, deep breath. "Maybe I'm just reading too much into this. I feel bad for Michelle. Let's try to have a good time and hope the weekend ends soon."

"Karen, do me a favor. Never be alone in the house. Be with me, Honoré, or Michelle. My coppy senses make me unwilling to trust anyone else."

Karen agrees. We try and relax while waiting for the dinner gong. We were informed that the dress code would be more informal. I choose charcoal-gray pants and a navy polo shirt. My dress shoes are polished to a high gloss. Karen steps into the black dress and jacket she bought in Ireland and wore to Lord O'Connor's party. She still takes my breath away. However, I'm reminded of the feelings associated with the tragic end of that night.

The gong sounds. Shoes click on the hard floor as we make our way to the dining room.

Mr. Butler is again at the door, handing out sealed envelopes. "Good evening." It comes with a slight bow. "My instructions are to ask that each clue remains closed until instructions are given."

We take ours. The room is configured with one large table in the center. One small table and a single chair are placed to one side. Monsieur Bres is already seated at it. We make eye contact. I nod acknowledgement, and he does the same. My gaze reaches Honoré, who indicates two vacant chairs.

When all the guests are present, Monsieur Bres stands. "I do not wish to diminish the seriousness of our situation. First and foremost, I would like to remember our compatriot, Mr. Drew Taylor, a.k.a. Corey Ander, whose terrible accident is truly a sadness. He will be missed. Secondly, we are stranded here due to the weather and road conditions. My decision to continue with the contest is to provide some level of enjoyment and distraction. Each of your clues takes the form of a unique riddle. Solving it will lead to a second clue to be solved, that will in turn provide the name, motive, or weapon of a possible suspect. Please help yourselves to some dinner. The gong will sound when you are welcome to open your clue. Enjoy."

He sits down. Mr. Butler offers red or white wine to each guest. People begin filing toward the buffet line. Karen and I join them. Sliced ham and turkey, several types of bread, cheeses, a berry compote, pasta salad, boiled potatoes, a warm carrot and pea medley, and pickled vegetables make the main course. Marble sheet cake with chocolate frosting is the offering for dessert. I'm impressed with what the staff has done and am grateful. Karen is expressing this same idea to Michelle, who assures us she will pass it on to her father. Glasses of wine, eating, and reminiscing make the evening more enjoyable than anticipated.

The gong rings. Each guest opens their clue. With some lips silently moving, and with others mumbling out loud, looks of confusion or frustration are evident. Dr. Hurt's eyes light up. "Got it." He hurries out of the dining room.

Les Burn grumbles, "Funny, fire . . . of course . . . always with the fire." He releases a disgruntled huff and heads into the hall, but not before grabbing a bottle of wine off the table and bumping into the doorframe as he exits.

Karen rolls her clue over and over in her hand. I can feel the wheels in her head turning. "The office!" comes her triumphant response.

"Huh?"

"It is full of paper and full of ink. It is not a book, so what do you think? My guess is a printer, which is in the office. What does yours say?"

"Can you find something which has keys that open no locks, with space but no room, and allows you to enter but not go in?"

"I think the key words . . . sorry, no pun intended . . . are keys, space, and enter. So, my thought would be a computer keyboard. What do ya think?"

I grab Karen and kiss her. "I knew I married smart. Come on, let's head to the office."

Bill Ding slams his clue to the table. "This is stupid. I do not know why I am even here. I could be doing better things." He proceeds to look at the card again. Estelle Hertz sits next to him and begins comparing her clue to his.

"Honoré, have you solved it yet?" I ask.

A wicked smile creases his lips. "See for yourself, *mon ami*." I turn his over and realize it's written in French. He laughs out loud. I do also. So much for my thinking that I might be smarter and figure his out.

"I will translate. 'People buy me to eat, but never eat me. What am I?'"

"I'd say something like utensils. You know, forks or knives," I reply.

Nodding, Honoré hurries to the kitchen. Karen and I head for the office. As we step into the hall, I notice Dr. Hurt coming in the front door. He's wet from the rain. Answering the question on my face, he states, "My riddle led me to the door. I checked inside and out, but no luck. I must have gotten the clue wrong. It is still raining though." He shakes off and returns to the dining room.

Karen and I proceed toward the office. Karen hesitates before going in. "I feel a little odd going through Monsieur Bres' things."

"He set the game, so it is what it is," I state, lifting the keyboard and retrieving my second clue. Karen looks around, above, underneath, and over all sides of the printer. Nothing. She opens the paper draw. There is something printed on the top page. "Ha. Got it! My second riddle is 'Soap and water, but it does not clean hands, used with Persil, Ariel, and many others.'"

I offer, "Dishwasher?"

"I know that Persil is a brand of laundry soap, so maybe a washing machine. Wherever that's located. What's yours say?"

"You will find a clue with tools used to eat. Hurry now, your hunt is almost complete." I grab her hand and move toward the kitchen. Crossing the hall, we nearly bump into Honoré, who says, "It was not utensils. It was a table. I found my second riddle taped under where I was sitting. Now I must go to the garage." With a jerk of his head toward the dining room, he adds, "He would make me go out in this rain." He walks away, muttering in French. I sympathize as he closes the front door. I turn the corner toward the kitchen hall when a horrendous shattering sound echoes from the living room. Someone screams. Karen and I pivot on our heels and head toward the noise. Estelle Hertz flings open the living room door, shouting, "Help! Please, someone!"

I run into the room, then stop abruptly. Karen bumps into my shoulder and gasps. Bill Ding is under the large wooden liquor cabinet. Alcohol, broken glass, and blood spread across the beige carpeting. His head and a single hand, still clutching the riddle, are the only body parts not covered by the massive piece of furniture. I step forward and check for a pulse on Bill's neck. Nothing. I face Karen and shake my head negatively. She pulls both of her hands over her mouth in disbelief. Dr. Hurt, Michelle, Jules, and Camille are at the door. I motion for them to stop. "Can you all wait in the dining room, please?" As they move, low-grade muttering is audible, but nothing I can make out. Suspiciously missing is Les Burn, our intoxicated firefighter. I'll worry about him later.

Estelle asks, "Is he . . . dead?"

"Yes. Can you tell me what happened?"

She responds shakily, "After dinner, we were comparing riddles. He was frustrated about his. So, I was helping him. The answers to his riddle and mine both seemed to be found in this room. He opened the doors on the cabinet while I went to the piano. Suddenly I heard him yell. When I turned around, it was falling, and he was trapped under it." She closes her eyes and lets out a sharp sob. Karen puts her arm around Estelle's shoulders. I reach down and remove the piece of paper from the victim's hand. It reads, "I have a neck, but no head. What am I?"

Estelle searches my face. "You know, like a bottle. I remembered seeing all the liquor in here the first night we arrived."

"So why are you in here?" I ask hesitantly.

"My riddle was 'What has eighty-eight teeth, but never brushes them?'" She nervously hands me her paper. "I play piano, and I know that it has eighty-eight keys. So, we both came in here to look."

I make eye contact with Karen. "Please find Honoré. I'll stay here with the victim. Estelle, could you please go to the dining room and wait there until I come for you?" Estelle nods and sniffles as she slowly leaves the room. Karen is right behind her, closing the door as she leaves.

I move closer to examine the back of the cabinet. There are holes drilled for screws to secure it to the wall. However, there aren't any screws protruding from the wooden back or any other means to secure it. Why not? I pull my phone out and photograph the scene from all angles. Annoyingly it dawns on me that Karen has been gone a long time. How hard could it be to find Honoré? He couldn't have gone far.

The door flings open, and Karen bursts in, dripping wet, panting, "Dan, come quick. I know that Honoré went to the garage. I heard the cars running, but all the doors are locked, and I couldn't find a way in."

I push past her, running. Michelle sees me. "What's wrong?"

Karen stops. I don't. I make my way through the downpour to the garage. Smoke is coming from under the overhead door. I try the side entry. Locked! I shoulder-slam the door. It's solid and doesn't relent. A second and then a third slam are needed before it crashes against the inside wall. Exhaust fumes hit my nose and throat. Coughing, eyes burning, I call for Honoré. No response. It's too dark to make out much. I slide my hands on the walls around the door, looking for an opener. My fingers bump against it. Pressing it several times to no avail, I then drop to my knees and grope my way. A car to my left. I reach up to pull the door open and shut off the engine. Locked! Karen is screaming my name. Michelle is crying out for Honoré. Moving forward, choking, eyes tearing, inching along, sweeping my arm in front of me. This is taking too long. Where is he? Is he even in here? The floor feels gritty. I continue creeping until I touch something. I run my hand across it. It's large, soft, and warm. Honoré. I grab his foot. Pulling, tugging, yanking, I inch us to the exit. Karen is there. She grabs my shirt and pulls me forward onto the driveway, into the rain.

I land on all fours and suck in a massive damp, clean, and cold breath of air. I spin around to check on Honoré, who is only a matter of feet beyond me. Dr. Hurt leans over him, checking, saying something I can't hear as my coughing and the pounding of my heart in my ears drown it out. Karen is holding me and crying. I pat her hand. Honoré's lying on his side, choking spasms seizing him. Michelle is kneeling beside him, stroking his arm, and talking. Our coughs synchronize, begin to slow, and near-rhythmic breathing begins.

That's when I feel the rain. A chill seeps into my body. Dr. Hurt makes eye contact. I wave him off and stand up. Karen has her arms around me. She shivers. Fear, cold, or both? Honoré's eyes open, and a faint smile crosses his lips. He breathes deeply, shudders, and coughs slightly. The doctor and I help him stand and support him as we trudge our way to the house, all of us completely soaked. Right now, I could use the rain to stop. I'm really over this weather and this weekend.

What a sight this group must be, coming through the front door. Hair soaked, clothes sticking to various body parts, squeaking shoes, dripping massive amounts of water on the floor, not caring about it. A gasp from the dining room entry grabs my attention. Estelle Hertz steps into the hall. Shock covers her face. Wide-eyed, she searches from face to face, then asks, "What happened?"

Replies from several of us simultaneously blend into a cacophony of undistinguishable answers. Once at the dining table, Dr. Hurt and I help Honoré into a chair, then proceed to drop into available seats ourselves with loud twin sighs. Karen hovers over my shoulder. Michelle is kneeling in front of her husband. Mugs of hot tea are presented to us by Mr. Butler and gratefully accepted. Several gulps into it, I feel some warmth in my fingers and the ability to form reasonable thoughts again.

I start to direct a question to Honoré. "Can you tell me . . ."

Monsieur Bres interrupts. "What has happened?"

Bewilderment then anger flash through Honoré's eyes, and it's reflected in his response. "What? You are going to stand there and act innocent? You know exactly what happened. You did this!"

Monsieur Bres answers, but not in English. Their exchanges get more heated. Both speak rapidly and loudly in French. I don't understand the words, but I can guess, given the body language and facial expressions. Michelle puts herself between the two most important men in her life. Tears stream down her face as she pleads with both. Neither heed. I grab Honoré before he says something he can't take back if he hasn't already.

"Hey, we need to get changed and focus on the victim in the living room," I say.

He shakes his head as if to bring himself out of his one-on-one argument. "Victim . . . in the living room? What *are* you talking about? What victim?"

I pat his chest. "There's been another accident." I wink at him.

A slight pause before the realization occurs to him. "Ahhh" escapes his lips.

I continue, "Let's head upstairs. We both could use a hot shower and dry clothes. We'll meet in the living room when we're done. There's another scene to investigate."

His shoulders drop, and he moves toward the door. Monsieur Bres has disappeared from the room, again. I didn't see where he went. How does he do that? Taking Karen's hand, we head upstairs.

CHAPTER 8

Karen offers me the bathroom first. She plans on immersing herself in a hot bath and possibly surfacing in a day or two. I appreciate the gesture. Once I'm in the shower, hot water hits my body. I concur with staying in there until the weekend is over. It takes all my self-talk of needing to investigate another tragic accident and preserve vital evidence in the living room to force me to turn the shower off. I *can* do this.

Dried off and dressed, I ask Karen to sit with Michelle in their room before I head downstairs. Honoré is already in the living room. His mouth gapes open. He attempts to speak, but full sentences escape him. "What? How? When?"

"Yup, as we know the where, the only thing missing is who," I quip.

"I will get my evidence kit. I am not sure how much in supplies I have left. I thought the last accident was going to be it for the weekend," he states.

While he's gone, I review the pictures on my phone. Something is different. Moving around the scene, I compare what I see now to what I have on my phone. A hand on my shoulder causes me to jump. "What?"

Honoré laughs out loud. "I am sorry, *mon ami*. I was asking what has been done to process the area."

"Sorry, I didn't hear you. Karen and I arrived seconds after hearing the crash. I photographed the room, but now it's different."

He knits his eyebrows together. "What is different?"

Scrolling through my pictures, I enlarge the one of the cabinet back. His eyes dart between the scene and my phone. Suddenly his mouth drops open. I nod in agreement. The screws securing the cabinet to the wall, missing in my pictures, are now clearly lying on the floor at the base of the cabinet.

"Someone realized their mistake and came back to correct it," Honoré says angrily. His lips press firmly together.

"I don't think this was an accident. However, was Bill Ding the intended victim?" I speculate.

Honoré doesn't answer. We fingerprint the outside of the cabinet. No fingerprints. Curiouser and curiouser.

I attempt to lift the cabinet, but it doesn't move. "How are we going to lift this? It's solid mahogany." I look at Honoré.

"A car jack, maybe. I will ask Mr. Butler to bring one from the garage. I have had enough of that place for one night," Honoré states. I agree with that thought.

Honoré leaves to find Mr. Butler. I re-photograph the area. Honoré returns, and a short time later, so does Mr. Butler, a car jack in hand. Apparently, no one wanted him dead, at least not tonight. I mentally slap myself for thinking that and shake off the shudder of how close Honoré came. Butler stays to help us raise the cabinet and move the body. He excuses himself to find the cart used for Corey Ander.

The three of us transport the body to the winery refrigerator. Honoré pulls the key from his pocket and opens the lock. Bill Ding's body is placed next to Corey Ander's. We step out. Honoré secures it closed and nods to Butler, who quietly heads back to the mansion.

"What about interviewing the guests and staff?" I inquire.

Looking at his watch, Honoré sighs. "It is after one o'clock in the morning. I am exhausted, angry, and between you and me, scared. I want some sleep. I *need* some sleep to collect my thoughts and focus. Tomorrow."

I acquiesce. We walk to the dining room to find out that our suspects must have gone to bed. Well, it's not like they can escape. Suddenly I'm tired. I want to lie down, hold Karen close, and hopefully wake up from this nightmare. Honoré and I part at the top of the stairs. Karen is already in bed when I step in. So much for not being alone. Imploring my best ninja skills, I get undressed and slide into bed. She rolls over and puts her arm across my chest. I don't remember anything after that.

My eyes open, and unfortunately, I'm still in the mansion. I hear Karen in the bathroom. I throw my legs out from under the blankets and sit up. Keenly aware of a headache, I ponder if it's too early to start drinking alcohol. I resign myself to searching for some aspirin. A quick glance outside reveals nothing has changed. Pouring rain, again!

Karen steps into the bedroom, bathed and dressed. "Hey, how are you?"

"Fine," I reply slowly.

"Can I get you something? I'll run down for a cup of coffee if that would help."

I laugh slightly. "Thanks, but no. I need to get up and meet Honoré."

I grunt as I stand and head for the bathroom. My body feels as if it's aged a decade overnight. A shower and fresh clothes help to revive me. Karen is sitting on the bed when I finish. We head down to breakfast. Honoré, Michelle, Jules, and Camille are at the table. Karen and I fill our plates. The smells of coffee, bacon, and scrambled eggs remind my stomach how long it's been since we last ate. Sips of coffee hit the back of my mouth, then slide down my throat. Its warmth and comfort bring me back enough to observe that the room is awkwardly quiet. Guests seem preoccupied one way or another. Les Burn tucks into a full plate without reservation, barely raising his head. Duane Pipe is a close second, chomping noisily. No guilt over the deaths, or oblivious to the implications? Estelle Hertz seems shaken as she pushes the little she's taken around her plate. Dr. Hurt has opted for just a cup of tea, which he stares into. Is he divining answers to the situation, forming a safety plan or an alibi? Jules rolls a cup of coffee between his hands absentmindedly. Karen, Michelle, and Camille have opted for a continental breakfast. Silently I ask the other guests, "Are you a murderer or potentially the next victim?" Honoré and I fuel up with more protein, less carbs. No naps today.

I finish my first cup of coffee and waste no time filling a second. Honoré fully formulates a plan to make sure we've processed the scene, then we'll interview the guests and staff.

I whisper to Karen, "Please stay with Michelle today. I don't want you alone, and she's the only other person I trust. We'll take a statement from you later." Karen nods acknowledgement.

Honoré announces to the room that each person needs to be available for interviews later today.

Les Burn slurs, "Not like anyone is leaving." His voice trails off, speaking more to himself. Is he drunk already? How? The liquor cabinet was destroyed. Maybe he packed his own supply.

Honoré snaps his head in the direction of the living room, my cue that we're heading over there. A third cup to go. We walk through the living room. Pictures compared, fingerprinting, and search of trace elements completed, Honoré slaps me on the back. "I will speak to my father-in-law about securing this evidence and using his office to conduct the interviews. This will be difficult."

I do a second assessment while he's gone and am confident we've done all we can given the limits of our resources.

When Honoré returns, we set up in Monsieur Bres' office at the massive desk with a pad of paper each and a supply of pens. Estelle Hertz is first. Her eyes are red and swollen, her hair a mess. She wrings her hands and cries on and off, using the palm of her hand to wipe her tears. "How could that have happened? I just keep thinking I could have received that clue, then I would be the one." She gasps for breath. "That poor man. It was terrible."

"You saw the cabinet fall?" I ask.

"I was searching around the piano when I heard a loud creak and Bill shouted, 'Oh, no!' He sounded panicked. I looked up. He took one step back, but it was too late, the cabinet was falling." She releases a deep sob. "I am a nurse, and the sight of him under the cabinet, his eyes open . . ." Estelle closes her eyes as if to make the vision stop. She reiterates much of what she said the night before. She stands to leave, then stops. "Wait, last night Les Burn was leaving the living room as I was about to go in. I remember because when I reached for the doorknob, the door flew open and scared me. He was muttering something like 'He thinks he is funny, but he will be sorry about it.' He pushed past me. He smelled of alcohol. I thought maybe he was looking for more to drink in the liquor cabinet, but then maybe his clue led him there."

Honoré and I thank her. Once she closes the door behind her, we discuss the information. If Les Burn was getting a bottle for his use, did he open the cabinet? If he did, why didn't it fall on *him*? Was he the intended victim and Bill Ding was unlucky? Why weren't Les' fingerprints anywhere on the cabinet?

We agree to speak to Les Burn next. If he's not drunk, he does smell like one. That sour combination of body order and old alcohol escapes through his pores. Honoré asks him to recount his movements from the night before, especially after dinner.

He cocks his head and stares over my shoulder. I'm ready to turn around to see if the answer is there when he states, "I got my riddle. The monsieur thinks he is funny. The answer is 'fire.' I am a firefighter, so the joke is always 'fire.' He is not clever."

Honoré knits his eyebrows together and summarizes, "So you read the riddle you were given and felt the answer was 'fire,' and you went to the living room because . . . why?"

Les releases an exasperated sigh. "Fire in the fireplace in the living room."

"Do you still have the paper the clue was on?" I ask.

"No." He slams his fist on the desktop. "He is not smart. He is not funny. I do not do what he says. I threw the riddle in the fire." The last word comes with a visual reenactment.

"What do you mean you don't do what he says?"

Les waves a dismissive hand. "I am not saying more. I will speak with Monsieur Bres first."

Shaking his head, Honoré focuses back on his questions. "Okay, so you get to the fireplace. Were you right? Was your second clue on or near the fireplace?"

"*Sì,* the second riddle was about cold. I thought it meant the refrigerator, so I went to the kitchen. Nothing. *He* is not serious about giving the money."

I jump in. "When you were in the living room last night, did you open the liquor cabinet?"

"No. I took a bottle of wine from the dining room. When I was done in the kitchen, I went to my room to drink it."

"Where were you when the cabinet fell over?" Honoré questions.

Les snaps his answer. "I said *my room.* I do not hear the crash. I am not involved." He puts his head down on the desk. "I must lie down. I am very tired." He stands up and heads for the door.

"We're not done with our questions," I call after him. He opens the door and lets himself out, oblivious to my statement. I look at Honoré, who throws up his hands. "I guess he was done. Dr. Hurt next?"

Dr. Hurt sits down. He is perfectly polished. Crisp navy-blue polo shirt, charcoal-gray pleated dress slacks, and high-shined black dress shoes.

"Can you account for your movements last night?" Honoré asks.

"I was in my room most of the afternoon. I came down for dinner. After reading my clue, I was convinced I had it right and acted upon it."

I look at the doctor. "Do you still have your clue?"

He pulls a folded piece of paper from his front pant pocket and hands it to me. I unfold it and read it aloud. "'People often knock me, but you'll lock me up before you go.' So, what did you think it meant?"

His eyes search my face and Honoré's. "A front door. You know, 'knock me' and 'lock me up before you go.' Get it?" We nod.

"I went to the front door, but there was nothing on the inside, so I went outside. I did not find anything. Either I was wrong, or it was the wrong door, or maybe Monsieur Bres was just playing a joke on whoever got that riddle to see if the person would actually go outside in this weather."

"Did you go into the garage last night?" I inquire.

Dr. Hurt looks confused. "No, why would I?" Then his eyes widen as if he just realized that we're accusing him of the attack on Honoré. A sharp tone creeps into his voice. "No. No, I did not have anything to do with what happened to you last night." His glare could have left burn marks on Honoré's face.

A sly grin creases Honoré's lips. "We are not saying you did. However, you were the only one who was wet shortly after dinner. You can see how that would be of interest to us."

"I was wet because that is what the riddle said." His finger hits the desk with emphasis. "I do not like what you are saying."

I don my best innocent look and say to Honoré, "Are we saying he did anything? I don't think we're doing *that*. Do *you* think we're doing that?"

Slowly shaking his head from side to side, Honoré answers breathlessly, "No, we are not." Dr. Hurt sets his jaw and gives us a condescending look.

I sheepishly smile and say to the doctor, "Did anyone come past you while you were outside, or did you see anyone out there?"

His answer is curt. "No. Are we done?"

"For now. Thank you," replies Honoré.

Dr. Hurt closes the door a little too hard on his way out.

Laughing out loud, I say, "I was waiting for you to say, 'We may have further questions, so don't leave town.'"

Honoré lets out a full-on belly laugh. He sucks in a deep breath and releases it. "*Mon ami*, what are we doing? I do not know any of these people or why anyone would want to hurt them. I know my father-in-law does not like me, but why try and kill me? At some point we will have to interview him too."

I chuckle nervously as I rub my fingertips on my temples. "Who's next?"

Duane Pipe plops down in the chair. "What's going on here? This is creepy. Are we all victims, just waiting to be killed? You guys know anything?"

"Right now, we're treating both deaths as accidents. Do you remember what you did last night?"

He looks at me skeptically. "Got my clue, thought the old man was being ironic with the answer being 'a shower.' You know, Duane Pipe." Most of his statement is in finger quotes.

I don't know if Honoré is lost, but I am and say so. "I don't understand. What are you talking about?"

He pulls a paper from his shirt pocket. He's actually wearing the same shirt he had on at dinner. He tosses it at me.

I pick it up. "Okay, 'A place where water falls down like rain, after it falls on you it goes down the drain.'"

Duane states, "See? You know, Duane Pipe, or should I say 'drainpipe'?" Like a shower. Went to my room and looked all over my bathroom, didn't find anything, wasn't going to go through other people's bathrooms, but maybe there's a shower for the staff or something. I was coming back downstairs to ask when I heard the crash and saw people running to the living room."

"What didja do then?" I ask.

"I went to the doorway. You and your wife were there, Estelle was screaming. I don't do blood and stuff. I ran to my room. Sorry, it's not very brave, but I would've passed out."

Honoré blinks several times. "Okay. Did you see anyone outside or coming or going through the front door?"

"No, I was so freaked out that someone would ask me to help with the guy that I just ran."

"Well, if you think of anything else, let us know." Duane is released. I throw my pen down, lean back in my chair, and run my fingers through my hair. "So far, we got nothing."

CHAPTER 9

Honoré and I decide to search Bill Ding's room. Entering the room, it's surprisingly neat. Clothes folded in drawers or hanging in the closet. Empty luggage stacked in a corner. Toiletries organized on the bathroom shelf. The search doesn't uncover any personal documents. No wallet, passport, or anything that reveals his name. He would've had to have something. Did he leave them with Monsieur Bres for safekeeping? Why?

"I need to speak to my father-in-law as to who these people are."

I inquire, "Are you goin' alone?"

"The buddy system is best when entering the lion's den," responds Honoré with hesitation.

"Family situations are some of the deadliest in policing," I say, shooting him a grin. He slaps me on the back while laughing heartily. We enter the hall and learn from Butler that Monsieur Bres is having lunch in his sitting room. Oops, we missed that meal. The elevator previously used to move our victims down to the passageway to the winery now takes us up to Monsieur Bres' private suite. The elevator opens, and we're greeted with a massive medieval-style wooden door. Cool! A place for the master of the castle to retreat to. Honoré knocks, then waits. *"Entrez"* comes the response.

Opening the door, we walk into a huge room with a single low-watt light revealing oversized furniture, a bookcase on every wall, and a chandelier of fighting lances that engulfs the ceiling. The drapes drawn make it dark and cool. Okay, weird to eat lunch in near darkness, or has he finished and was napping? Monsieur Bres sits in a chair near the windows, elbows resting on the armrests, fingertips pressed against each other. He is a shadowy figure, where the most distinctive feature are the whites of his eyes, which appear to glow in the room. *"Oui."*

Honoré clears his throat. *"Patron,* I am sorry we are bothering you, but we have questions."

The seated figure nods. Honoré continues, "Can you give us some background on each of your guests and why you invited them?" I'm poised to take notes.

He replies, "Some of the guests are apparent. You, my daughter and son, his wife, and friends of yours. As for the others, they are business associates. You know that I am stepping away from the daily business operations. Jules will take over. The consultants and their insights directed many of my deals over the years. I wanted to thank them and say good-bye. My birthday was an excuse to throw a final, big party. Now it is marked with sadness."

Honoré continues, "We were in Bill Ding's room. There is no identification at all. Did he leave it with you?"

"Oui, his passport and some confidential papers he was working on are locked in my safe. His real name is William

Wright. I have used his architectural firm on many of my building projects. He was efficient and used local labor on projects that benefited him and the community."

"Any known enemies or a reason for anyone to kill him, especially anyone here?" Honoré asks.

"In business, we all make enemies, real or not. People who think it was not fair who got the contract, how they got the contract, or if any accidents were the firm's fault."

My ears perk up. "Accidents? Was someone hurt at one of his sites, and do the family members blame him? Could one of them be here now?"

Cold eyes turn to me. "*Non*" is his reply.

Honoré coughs. "But why these specific people? You must know hundreds."

"Each person was chosen for a specific reason. Drew Taylor, or as you knew him, Corey Ander, catered all my events. He was the chef behind the amazing weekend menu. However, without him or the additional staff it requires, it cannot be accomplished." A long sigh escapes him. "As for the others, five years ago, Dante Fuoco investigated a fire at one of my buildings in Italy. His report highlighted severe flaws in the insurance company's claim that it was arson. They ended up paying out one hundred percent. If it had not been for him, that loss would have cost me millions. I have used his expertise on fire prevention ever since. A weekend was the least I could do for him."

"This Dante, is that Les Burn's true name?" Those eyes turn to me, again. I shake it off. "Could you spell the last name, please?"

Slow, deliberate letters are enunciated. "F-U-O-C-O."

I mutter, "Thank you."

"*Patron*, the others?" Honoré questions.

Monsieur Bres' eyes blaze with intensity and turn to Honoré. "I have your confidence? My family must *never* know."

Honoré agrees. "What you tell us stays here." I'm not ready to agree, but this isn't my family. What's he gonna say that they can't know about? Will this be a confession? Is he behind these "accidents"?

"Nearly ten years ago, while on a business trip to Canada, I had a medical emergency and was raced to the local hospital. The senior doctor on staff made a diagnosis and was about to send me to surgery when a young intern challenged that diagnosis. He stood his ground, requested an MRI, and was correct. Surgery would have killed me. I am forever in his debt."

"Dr. Hurt?" Honoré asks.

"*Oui*, Dr. Saeed Virk."

I add, "May I ask what the diagnosis was?"

Monsieur Bres waves his hand dismissively. "That part is not important. Just to say that I have used the doctor for all my health needs since. His nurse, Sue Jannsen, is going to retire. I wanted them both to understand the depth of my gratitude. Tomorrow night, Dr. Virk is going to present his retirement gift to his nurse. Please keep that secret. This has not been a weekend of joy, but I would like him to have that moment if he still wishes."

Honoré and I agree to keep what has been shared between us. It's a bit disappointing. No confession from him. He seems to have nothing but respect for his guests. Strangers brought together as a thank-you. Are these weird, random accidents? I still don't believe it. Then who's behind them, and why? Is there a mysterious "Mr. or Ms. X" that no one would think capable of these things because we don't know their motives? Curiouser and curiouser.

Honoré pushes. "Then there is Duane Pipe. What is his real name?"

"Thomas."

Looking up from my notes, I ask, "Is that a first name or a last?" I wasn't prepared for the answer.

"Both."

Skeptically, I question, "His name is Thomas Thomas? You're joking, right?"

"*Non*, Thomas means twin, and he has a twin sister. His father thought it was funny. He may not have been original, but he was my best friend. Prior to his death, he sold his company to me with the provision I find a place for his son. I did. He became an apprentice in a plumbing firm I own in Cape Town."

"Can you think of anyone here that would want to hurt your guests, including *me*?" Honoré says.

Monsieur Bres flatly replies, "*Non*. I know you will not believe me, but I did not lock you in the garage. My daughter would have been sad at losing you."

Honoré bows in acquiescence, but I'm not so sure. I'm keeping my options open on everyone there. He pushes on. "Can you tell us about your staff?"

"Marie Dubois, my housekeeper, has been with me twenty years or more and runs the household. *C'est magnifique*. Louis Moreau is the vintner. He was here when I bought the place.

Only James Butler is new. I hired him when my former butler's vision began to fade."

"I remember his arriving one or two years ago, I think,"
Honoré states.

"*Oui.*"

"Where was he hired from?" I ask.

A sly smile crosses the monsieur's lips. "I lured him away
from the house of a business associate. He trained at the British
Butler Institute, had exceptional references, and wanted a
change from living in England."

Wow, he does that to someone he knows? I hope I never
cross him. Wonder if his money often gets him what he wants.

We both thank him and head back to the office. Karen and
Michelle are waiting there with sandwiches and hot coffee.
Kisses are bestowed to the proper spouses for their thoughtful-
ness. Between bites, we review what we know. Michelle offers
the bulletin board that she and Karen started as part of the
murder mystery weekend. We agree it would be a great way
to organize the information, much the same way as they had it
with suspects, motives, etc. She heads out to retrieve it.

I inform Honoré, "Karen was with me all day. Last night,
our clues took us to the same rooms. Who do we still need to
question?"

He guffaws. "I do not suspect you or Karen. Same with
Michelle and I because of the garage episode." He shudders.
"We will talk to Jules and Camille. They did not play along. I
cannot believe they would be involved. Now let us speak with
the staff." Michelle is back with the board, note cards, and
markers in hand.

Honoré brings in Marie, the housekeeper. Marie is speaking in French; Honoré translates. She explains that she was in the kitchen cleaning up after dinner and preparing food for meals the next day. She confirms that the Italian man came in, looked around and in the refrigerator, muttered something, then stomped upstairs with a bottle of wine in his hand. Mr. Butler was helping her after dinner. She denies seeing anyone or anything suspicious in or around the kitchen.

After Marie leaves, Michelle speaks to Honoré in French. The tone leads me to believe she is upset that we questioned Marie.

Karen inquires, "Everything okay?"

"*Oui*," Michelle says through a tight smile. Honoré casts his eyes to the floor. Karen looks at me with worry in her eyes. I ditto the concern that the investigation has touched a nerve with Michelle and that it'll put Honoré in a difficult position.

"Butler next?" I ask. Honoré nods without eye contact. I find Butler in the hall and request he join us. He declines to sit in the chair offered.

I lead the questioning. "Can you tell me how long you've been with the household?"

"Twenty months, sir."

"Can you account for your movements last night until the incident in the living room?"

"I helped set up for dinner, then was at the dining room door handing out clues for the evening. During the meal, my responsibilities included removing used plates, utensils, and dinnerware, serving the wine, and generally making the evening run smoothly while assisting Marie, as we are without proper staff levels."

"I didn't notice you in the area when the cabinet fell. Do you remember where you were?"

"In the kitchen, sir. Assisting with the cleanup and preparation for today. Mr. Burn came in looking for something, but no one else did. When the crash occurred, I was not clear as to where in the house the noise came from. I first went to the dining room, then into the hall where the crowd was gathered at the living room door. Will that be all, sir?"

I dismiss him. "For now. Thank you." He bows his head and backs out of the office.

I rub the back of my neck. "Well, Marie and Butler alibi each other and Les Burn. We still need to talk to Jules and Camille."

Michelle snaps. "Why? They did not do this terrible thing."

Honoré pats her arm, which she yanks away from him. Intense and rapid French erupts between the couple. I step toward them. Honoré waves me off. Awkwardness fills the room. Karen shifts in place, looks at me, and thrusts her head in the direction of the hall. We step out of the office, closing the door.

Several minutes pass before Michelle opens the door. "I am sorry. This has not been the weekend I wanted for you. Please forgive me." Honoré stands quiet and stoic. His body language reveals no emotion.

Karen hugs Michelle. "There's nothing to forgive. It's been stressful for everyone. We have some time before dinner. Would you be able to find a good bottle of wine and bring it to our room? Let's have a drink and talk as old friends, not investigators, huh?"

Michelle smiles weakly. Michelle and Honoré move toward

the passageway leading to the winery. We can't stop the questioning now. We need to talk to people while the events are fresh in their minds and before they compare notes with others.

I turn to Karen, but she holds up her hands. "Let it go, Dan. Worry about the rest of the interviews later. Our friends are more important." She turns and heads up the stairs. I have little choice. I appreciate Michelle's feelings, as this involves her family, but it doesn't mean I'm not annoyed. I trudge behind Karen. Scenarios roll around in my brain. It isn't right to stop. Each person here is a potential suspect with a motive to not be caught. I review what's been said up to now. With enough time, even Karen could be suspicious. I laugh to myself. I promise to be a friend for now, but my guard will remain firmly up.

CHAPTER 10

Once in the room, Karen gives me a hug. "I know this isn't what you want to be doing, but I think it's what we need now." She doesn't wait for a response, but instead straightens the room when a knock interrupts. Honoré, Michelle, Jules, and Camille are at the door with bottles of wine, glasses, and a platter of cheese and crackers.

"Perfect," Karen says with a smile. We sit on the bed. Jules retrieves two chairs from their room for himself and Honoré. Camille and Michelle settle in the chairs in our room.

Jules sets about opening the bottles. "How is the investigation? Have any suspects?"

A palpable silence befalls the room. Jules looks from face to face. "Did I say something wrong? Am I not to ask?"

Michelle sighs and drops her shoulders. "No, I am the problem. I do not like to see people I love questioned like criminals. I have been cruel to my dear husband for just trying to solve these accidents." She has tears in her eyes. "I am sorry, *mon amour*."

Honoré leans over, kisses her head, and whispers something in French to her. She sits back, sniffling.

Glasses filled, we settle in to snack on the cheese and crackers when Jules perks up. "You have not questioned me.

How do you know that I did not do these things? Or Camille? Maybe she is, as you say, a dark widow?"

"Black widow?" I ask.

Laughing, Jules responds, "Yes, a black widow."

Camille's eyes widen as she objects. "I am not that. I do not know anything about these terrible things." Jules pats her hand, cooing something in French.

Honoré looks to Michelle, who nods affirmatively.

He starts, "What can you tell me about the people that are here for the weekend?"

Jules cocks his head to one side. "I have met some of them. William, or Bill Ding, worked on several of our buildings. My father really liked his cost. Always the lowest. Drew . . . umm, Corey Ander, catered most of my father's events, like this time. I think Drew did something mean to another restaurant or had a problem with a chef. Ask my father, he will know. Dante, the fire person, has come to some of our buildings to speak on fire prevention and safety. He seems angry many times, or drunk, but my father hires him." Jules shrugs. "I do not know why the doctor, the nurse, or the plumber guy are here or how my father knows them."

Camille remarks sarcastically, "I do not know any of them as my father-in-law and husband do not include me in the business." Jules shoots a menacing look at her.

I jump in. "Can you both account for your movements last night?"

"Camille and I were in our room after dinner. We are not part of the murder mystery. Camille read and then went to sleep. I had paperwork to finish until I went to bed."

Camille adds, "You were gone for a while from our room."

Jules eyes burn when looking at Camille, who visibly shrinks in her chair. "I needed my briefcase from my car."

My head snaps up, as does Honoré's.

Camille mumbles softly, "It was in our room before dinner."

"You were in the garage last night? Were you the one who tried to *kill* me?" Honoré roars and starts for Jules, who backs up until he hits the wall. Honoré's face is mere inches away from Jules. "Answer me. Were you?"

Jules is physically shaking and stuttering without cohesion. "I . . . I . . . I . . . no. Nothing . . . I." He changes to speaking rapidly in French. It's unclear if his explanation makes more sense. Michelle's face looks as if she's been slapped.

"What's he saying?" I ask, facing Honoré, throwing my hands up.

"*Non?*" Honoré exclaims in an exaggerated voice. He steps back, and his body visually relaxes. Looking at the floor, Jules releases a shaky breath as he responds in French. Camille has a queer smirk on her lips. What's that about? Did he reveal something embarrassing, that he did try to kill Honoré or someone else?

Honoré turns on his heels. "He is not the person we are looking for."

"What did he say? Was he in the garage? Did he do or see something or someone?" I pepper him with questions.

"He was not in the garage. He went to the winery to see Louis, the vintner" comes his answer.

Michelle is picking at a blanket on the bed.

"And? What was he doing there? Will Louis provide him with an alibi for the time you were trapped, or when the cabinet fell?" I'm not going to let it go.

"Enough! This is my family, not yours. It does not matter. It has nothing to do with our investigation."

I'm about to argue that without knowing what Jules said, I can't decide if it has something to do with the investigation or not, when the dinner gong rings.

Michelle abruptly stands. "There is the gong. We need to go and get ready for dinner." She pats my arm. "Please stop questioning my brother." They all leave our room.

Turning to Karen, fuming, I ask, "What the heck did he say that got everyone so upset?"

"Dan, I don't know, but for now leave it alone. You can talk to Honoré later when you're both cooler. There is something going on with the family, I can feel it. The optimal word being family. It's theirs. Please, just slow down, Detective." She kisses my cheek.

"I don't like the secrets. I'm gonna jump in the shower and try to relax before dinner."

Standing in the shower, the warm water running over my head, I breathe in and out, telling myself that there could be a perfectly innocent reason Jules went to see Louis. Maybe he's doing something behind his father's back with the wine. Trying a new vintage, or marketing, or even focusing on the winery while neglecting his father's business interests. All would lead to some conflict with Monsieur Bres. He's not a man who accepts not getting his way. I plan to speak to Louis either with Honoré or without if I must. I start to feel better and decide my wife and friends are the reasons we're here. I need to be a better guest and hope the authorities can arrive soon. Turning off the water, I dry off, dress, and let Karen know my plan to just enjoy the moment with our good friends. Her smile and hug reward me.

We step into the hall and meet Honoré and Michelle. I smile and extend my hand. He shakes it. His shoulders relax, and he smiles back. Michelle and Karen quietly speak while we all head downstairs to the dining room. Once there, the smell of hot food gives me a shot of pleasure to my brain, not to mention my stomach. Butler bows acknowledgement; I return the gesture. Monsieur Bres is at his private table, makes eye contact, and nods, as do I. Jules and Camille have chosen to sit near the doctor, his nurse, and the plumber, who looks like a scared rabbit. His eyes dart around the room as if on guard against some unknown attack. The scene in our room has upset the family relationship. I hope they mend soon.

The fireman has distanced himself from everyone and instructs Butler to leave a bottle of wine for him.

My eyes dance over the buffet. Limited staff or not, Marie has outdone herself. Roast beef in gravy, cold salmon, fresh rolls, salad, quiche, slices of watermelon and cantaloupe, chocolate cake with chocolate frosting, and coffee. This is a form of bliss. Butler is pouring glasses of a burgundy wine.

I sit at the table with a mountain of food on my plate. "You'd think I hadn't eaten in a year," I say lightheartedly.

A belly laugh escapes Honoré. "The French way of life. Good food, good wine, and good friends."

Just as I tuck into my dinner, Monsieur Bres stands and

raises his hands. Voices fall silent, and the staff pause. "My dear guests, this has been a terrible weekend. Considering the events, I am suspending the murder mystery game. In lieu of the one million euros that had been offered, please submit the name of your favorite charity and a sizable donation will be made. Each of you will receive a gift from me in the form of bottles of wine from my winery." He bows and sits down. The room buzzes. I strain to catch conversations, but they're too low to make out.

Les Burn, uhm . . . Dante, slams his fist to the table, mumbling incoherently, "Lie . . . never . . . money . . . fire . . . not me." He stands, still rambling. "What you say is not true about the money. You lie. It is not right that you say that." He falls back into his chair and quietly sobs into the crook of his arm. Butler quickly moves to Dante's side and whispers to him. Dr. Virk moves toward him as well. Dante backhands Butler in the face, causing him to stumble back into the doctor. Honoré and I are on our feet, ready to assist. I understand that the thought of losing a million euros is difficult, but the man has barely been sober most of the weekend. He couldn't have truly thought he would win. He needs a serious intervention, but for now we need to get him into bed. I reach his left side as Honoré reaches his right. Both of us take an arm. Dante rears up and tears away, running for the hall. "I go. I will not stay with a liar." He's at the front door. I'm amazed that a drunk guy can move that fast. Honoré and I are right behind him, but too far to prevent him from opening the door and running into the rain. We don't bother to grab coats while in pursuit. Whatever anyone is saying is lost in the pouring rain. I'm tired of this weekend. In the low light, my eyes adjust to a shadow moving down the driveway. I slap Honoré on the arm. My knees were not made for this anymore, but I pursue him.

Half running, mostly sliding through the mud that is the driveway now, I continue. Honoré falls beside me but gets right up. I'm not sure if I'm propelling myself or the pitch of the driveway has me on a downward trajectory. The sudden sound of the river blocks all other sounds. Please tell me that Dante will have sense enough to not try to cross the broken bridge. I thought I was long past chasing stupid drunks. I slide to a sloppy stop twenty feet from the bridge, but too quickly, and Honoré slams into me from behind with an audible "umph," followed by "Where is he?" We slowly creep forward. Rain drips into my eyes as I set foot on mud covering a wooden plank. Either I'm screaming out loud or it could be just in my head. Dante is sidestepping his way along the railing, then vanishes from view. Honoré and I move to where he was last seen. We drop to our knees and look over the side. Vertigo washes over me . . . I hate heights. I *hate* heights. Honoré nudges me, forcing my eyes open. He's pointing to a single hand holding onto a wooden slat. I grab hold of a sleeve and use two hands to pull it while Honoré pulls me. The elbow clears the side, then a head and shoulder. Slowly, the rest of Dante's body is on the bridge. Honoré tugs until all of us are on solid ground. Panting, we lie there for a moment, facedown. I smell the wet earth and grass. Pushing myself onto my knees, then standing up, I reach a hand down to Honoré, who in turn reaches down for Dante. We position ourselves under each of his arms. Trudging, we fight our way back up the hill toward the house.

Karen and Michelle meet us and throw coats over our

shoulders. The motley band slugs to the front door. I feel like I've been outside for a week. Once inside and looking down, I see that I'm dripping across the harlequin tiles, but I'm too tired to stop for fear I won't get started again. We use the elevator. Michelle is supervising Honoré and yells orders to Mr. Butler to take Dante. Karen maneuvers me to our room. We don't stop until I'm in the shower with warm, glorious water cascading over me. I lean on the wall, close my eyes, and say, "I love you, Karen."

"Okay, I love you too. Let's get you out of those wet clothes. Dan, you have to help some."

It feels like a herculean task to pull my clothes off. Chills run through my body. I huddle as much of me as possible under the spray.

"Here, drink this," Karen orders, handing me a cup of something.

"What is it?"

"Coffee," she snaps.

"I love coffee." Warm sips trickle down my throat. I feel myself coming to.

"Yeah, yeah, I know. You okay? What were you thinking?"

"I wasn't. We don't need another victim" comes my breathless reply. "I'll just stand here a little more. I love Monsieur Bres' hot water heater."

Minutes pass before I have the energy to extricate myself from the shower. Stepping into the bedroom, I see dry clothes laid out for me. I start to dress when I make eye contact with Karen, who has tears in her eyes. "Don't do that again. I thought I lost you and Honoré."

I drop my head. "I'm sorry. It flashed through my mind to just let Dante go, but I'd regret it if something happened to him or Honoré, if he had tried to help and I could've prevented it. Sorry."

"It's one of the things I love about you. Your kind heart," Karen says, kissing me all over my face. I hold her close, painfully aware of how badly the situation might have ended.

Stepping back to look at me, Karen informs me, "The doctor was asked to check on Dante. Do you want him to check you too?"

I shake my head. "I'm good. In fact, I'm a little revved up. Let's walk downstairs. Maybe we'll find a deck of cards or something. I just don't want to be in this room right now."

Karen nods and takes my hand. We head to the office. I open the door, turn on the lights, and we step in. We start at opposite ends of the bookcases, searching for anything of interest that's written in English. The distinctive creak of wood catches my attention. Glancing at the office door, it hasn't moved. Karen is engrossed in a book. I step closer, and the floor lets out a small groan. I snicker to myself about old houses and their sounds. My "coppy senses" are suddenly up. I spin around and am face-to-face with Monsieur Bres, who says, through a tight smile, "*Bonsoir*. Can I help you find a good book?"

Flushed, I stutter, "Where did you come from?"

"This is my house, anywhere and everywhere."

"I'm sorry I didn't hear you come in," Karen says, approaching my side. She found something to read. I'm a little unnerved and decide not to look any longer. Taking her hand, I mumble a "good night" and head out of the office.

Once in the hall, Doctor Virk makes eye contact. "My nurse and I were able to get Dante into some dry clothes. He is sleeping off his latest binge. I could not find anything seriously wrong. A little hyperthermia, but he is resting comfortably now. I'll recheck him in the morning. Good night."

"I think that's a great plan for everyone. A little sleep and see how we are in the morning." He bows his head slightly and heads for the office. Looking for a book or business with Monsieur Bres? I pull Karen with me.

Once in the hall, Karen pulls her hand back. "Stop! Dan, what's wrong?"

"This place is getting to me. One second, there's no one, then suddenly Monsieur Bres is standing behind me. He walks like a cat. It's creeping me out."

Karen pats my chest. "Okay, let's go to bed. We can dream of sunshine and blue skies for tomorrow."

"Please, yes." We make our way to our room for the night.

CHAPTER 11

The morning starts gray, but silent. Absent is the sound of rain. Maybe our luck is changing, I silently hope. A quick shower and dress. Karen knocks on the bathroom door. "You okay?"

Opening the door, I reply, "Great! Did ya notice it's *not* raining?"

She turns her head toward the window and smiles. "Wait for me while I get ready, and we can go to breakfast together." The sound of the bath running allows me time to revisit the events of the last few days. I compile a list of "still needs to be done" for the investigation. First, I need some private time with Honoré. He knows things he's not sharing, especially about the family. How do I approach him so he knows he can trust me, whatever the secrets are? Do they implicate someone in the "accidents"? Maybe they're personal quirks that have nothing to do with the deaths. I just wish I knew what they were. I roll what I've witnessed over and over in my head. My frustration is turning to anger with the thought that Honoré doesn't trust me. The tension in my shoulders and neck is increasing when I hear "DAN."

"What?" I reply sharply, only to be looking at Karen.

"I've said 'I'm ready' three times, but it's like you didn't hear me."

I hug her. "I'm sorry. This whole situation has me turned around. May I accompany you to breakfast?"

She shoots me a sideways glance. "If you promise to be a husband, not a detective."

I hold up my hand. "I promise." We walk arm in arm downstairs to the dining room. Jules makes eye contact and quickly looks away. Karen heads for a table, I for the coffee, black and strong. It's slightly hot going down my throat and yet soothing. An audible "ahhhh" escapes my lips. A hearty chuckle from behind me snaps me out of my revelry. I spin around, face-to-face with Honoré. Handshakes done, Honoré says, "The rescue on the bridge last night, huh?"

"We're getting too old for that." Each of us has a hearty laugh, and we get in line for the buffet. Scrambled eggs, quiche, fresh fruit, sausages, and warm rolls fill my plate. At the table, Karen and Michelle are discussing the events of the night before. Both shoot us disapproving looks. Honoré and I look at each other, shrug, and snicker.

I'm ready to tuck into my food when I do a head count. All are accounted for except Dante and Dr. Virk, until the doctor walks in. He's dressed flawlessly in a black polo, black loafers, and black, pleated slacks. How does he do it? All the other guests, including myself, appear much more rumpled. Mental note to check on Dante. Sue, the nurse, stops by our table to say thank-you for our effort in saving Dante and that she thought us very brave.

The compliment, my plate empty, the second cup of coffee finished, I'm feeling content.

Honoré stands. "Dan, walk with me, please."

"O-O-Okay," I stutter in response.

He heads outside, grabbing a coat on the way. I follow his lead. The cool, damp air hits my face. Honoré is purposefully marching down the driveway. I slip on a patch of mud. Memories of last night flood back, and I stop abruptly. Honoré questions over his shoulder, "Are you alright?"

"A little reliving from last night." I shudder.

He walks to where I'm stopped and slaps my arm. "Time to get back on the horse, as you Americans say."

"I'm fine with getting back on the horse, but not so much the bridge."

He whispers, "Let us assess the condition of the bridge. We need to make an escape plan now."

My anxiety rises. I believe he's afraid, and not just of family secrets being revealed.

"Do you know something I should be aware of?"

He shakes his head. "*Non, mon ami.*" Facing me, he continues, "I must tell you something, but you must promise me to tell no one, not even Karen."

I reluctantly agree.

"When I met Michelle, I fell in love. She assured me her father would embrace me to the family. I remember being excited to meet him. It was not a good meeting. He was kind when Michelle was near, but when he spoke to me alone, he said all I wanted was her money and I would never be anything important. He offered me thirty thousand euros to never see Michelle again."

My mouth hangs open, until I force it to close. "I'm sorry, my friend. Obviously, you didn't leave or take the money."

"I loved her from the moment I saw her. I could not leave. I made sure we never took any money from him."

"What did Michelle say? You told her, right?"

"*Non.* She idolizes her father. Over the years, I tried to show him that I was not here for the money. Recently, I stopped trying. Now I point out to Michelle when he is rude to me. She makes an excuse for him."

"The fight on the night we arrived . . . I noticed you weren't offered an umbrella, even in the pouring rain, and when we met him in the library, he barely acknowledged you."

"*Oui.* When Michelle and I were in our room, we fought. She thinks I can be jealous of her father's success and attention to her. His dislike of me is the reason that led me to accuse him of being the one who tried to kill me in the garage."

"I'm so sorry. I appreciate why you want to escape. Let's make a plan."

We walk with added vigor to the bridge. Honoré heads to the edge, but I assess it from further away. I just can't do heights. He kicks it, steps on it, and it creaks. I'm starting to hyperventilate; my heart is racing.

"Could you just get off there, please?" I snap.

Honoré smiles at me. "I am sorry, my friend. I do not mean to make you nervous. The bridge is still connected on both sides. It would not hold the weight of a car, but a man in a harness on a rope may be able to walk across. He would be able to get to town and alert the authorities."

"It's an idea. The man will *not* be me, in case you're asking."

Honoré nods. "I weigh too much to be that man. Louis, the vintner, might be able. You and I together could hold him if something went wrong. Let us ask him." A sly smile creases his lips. "And he's not family."

The ascent up the driveway is much more arduous. I step into the hall and am aware of my mud-caked shoes. This time I remove them, as does Honoré. We plan to change our shoes and meet to go and speak with Louis about our plan.

Shoes exchanged, we head to the winery.

"Louis has an office. We can look for him there," Honoré says.

The office, on the ground floor of the winery, smells earthy with a hint of spice. A basic square room with a desk, chair, file cabinet, and maps and charts on every wall. Boxes, bubble wrap, cardboard-formed cartons, and general packing materials piled up in each corner. The desk is strewn with labels, invoices, and weather reports that are several days old. Three-ring binders fill a small wooden bookcase. Some stand upright, others are lying down, and a few sit half-opened on the floor. My eyes rove over the scene. I can't decide if Louis is disorganized or if the room was searched. I turn to Honoré, who anticipates my question. "It always looks like this."

No one is there. His room, one floor above his office, is a mess. It appears as if a struggle took place. Clothes everywhere, on the floor, bed, chair, dresser, and closet. The bed coverings mounted in the center of it. Plates with pieces of food, wine bottles, and glasses. I don't want to touch anything without gloves on for fear of catching some disease.

Honoré taps my arm. "He is not here. Let us go."

"Are you sure he isn't under a pile of stuff?" I say, kicking one of them.

He shakes his head and moves out of the room. I happily follow him.

We tour the winery itself, looking between vats and in shortage rooms, and conclude he must be in the vineyard. We each grab a pair of rubber boots and head out. After two hours of traversing the rows of vines, Louis is still missing.

Honoré stops, then leans over with his hands on his hips, sucking in deep breaths. "I do not know where he is. Let us go to the kitchen and ask Marie to let me know when Louis comes in for lunch."

Marie's busy chopping carrots. The room is warm, moist, and smells delicious. It wraps around me. Honoré is speaking to her in French. I'm looking into pots on the stove with lust in my stomach. There is a stew, vegetables being sautéed, beef browning, and a fresh loaf of bread on the counter.

Honoré taps my arm. "She says he never came in for breakfast."

"Maybe he's busy because of all the rain we've had."

"We should have found him then. Also, she says he has never missed a meal before, not even during harvest."

I offer a silent prayer that we don't have another "accident." We head back to the office, add Louis' disappearance to the board, and sit back, looking at the information.

"He may have decided to take a chance and cross the bridge to head into the village for help," Honoré throws out.

I face him with my eyebrows knit together. "You honestly believe he simultaneously came up with the same plan we did. Yeah, I don't think so."

Honoré snaps back, "It's the only plan there is at this time, so *yes*, he could have."

"What about waiting for cell or internet connection to return?"

"Reception is poor on good days. This weather makes it crap. If he *is* responsible for these "accidents," then he has not only tried to escape but is not going to the authorities when he gets to the village."

Heatedly I sit forward. "Why would he be responsible? We're not even sure he knew the victims, and he certainly didn't invite them."

"*Uggggggh,* I hate this place" erupts from Honoré. A cough is my poor attempt to quell my laughter. It's unsuccessful.

"Shut up," he responds before laughing, which migrates into a sigh.

"Because we can't find Louis, let's ask someone else to try crossing the bridge. What about Thomas, the plumber guy?"

"Yeah, that might work," Honoré agrees, standing up and heading for the door. I go with him.

Honoré knocks on Thomas' bedroom door.

"Who is it?" comes the reply. We announce ourselves. Minutes pass before we hear the slide bolt disengage. Thomas peeks out through a crack, then opens the door wider. Once inside, he hurriedly closes the door and slides the bolt to lock us in.

"Who were you expecting?" I question.

He twitches like he's been shocked. "No one. This place gives me the creeps. I do not feel safe *anywhere*. What do you want?"

We explain our plan. Thomas shakes all over. "No, no, I do not do heights, even if it is a chance to escape. I want to get out of here in one piece. Find someone else. Please leave." He unlocks the door, opens it, and waits for us to leave, which we do.

"Wow, he's really tightly wound," I comment once we're in the hall.

"What now?" Honoré asks.

"We keep looking for a volunteer. If we don't find one, I'll walk across, if enough people hold the rope," I offer.

"That is brave of you, *mon ami*. Let us see." We turn to walk back to the office when Dante stumbles out of his room. Hair standing upright, swaying in place, staring blankly at us for a moment, he turns and heads back into his room. Mental note checked; he's alive.

I look at Honoré, who opens his mouth to offer a suggestion. I cut him off. "Not a chance." A smile twitches at the corners of his mouth. Silently we walk back downstairs.

At the bottom of the stairs, we meet Karen and Michelle, who are coming out of the office.

Karen leans into Michelle. "Maybe we can ask these two *very* handsome detectives if they'll take a missing husbands report. I know we had husbands with us earlier, but now they've disappeared." Michelle laughs out loud.

"Ha, ha," I reply. "What were you two doing in the office?"

Michelle informs us that she and Karen were speaking with Monsieur Bres, who needed to work in the office this morning but is concerned at the disappearance of Louis.

"How does *he* know that Louis is missing? We just found out," Honoré questions.

Michelle looks at Honoré with indignation. "Papa learned from Marie that Louis did not come for breakfast and that you were looking for him. My papa worries as he thinks of all his staff as family. He would like a search organized. He fears that Louis may be sick or hurt and needs attention."

Honoré snaps, "Sure." His eyes flash more anger than agreement with her statement.

Karen jumps in. "We could ask for teams of two. Let's head to the dining room and approach people as they come in for lunch."

Honoré rolls his eyes at me. I reply with a sympathetic grimace. Michelle and Karen head into the kitchen to see if Marie or Butler need any assistance with setting up lunch.

Honoré states, "I need something strong to drink. I have a bottle of cognac in my room. I will get it."

"Man after my own heart," I call out after him. I find a table to sit at. My thoughts turn dark. What is the situation with Louis? Did he escape and is sending help? Is he hurt somewhere, hoping for help, or worse? Will we find another "accident" scene? Is he responsible for what has happened so far? My "coppy senses" don't think this will have a happy ending. Where is he?

CHAPTER 12

My whirling thoughts that have no answers, yet, are broken when Honoré returns with a bottle and glasses. Large portions are poured for each of us. We tip our heads back. The golden liquid burns, warms, and satisfies all the way down my throat. A joint "aaaahhh" escapes our lips.

I extend my arm for a fist bump with Honoré, who reciprocates. Karen and Michelle join us. Karen's eyes rove over the bottle and near-empty glasses. It's earlier than I normally have a drink; however, these are unusual circumstances, and the need to be a supportive friend allows for it. Disapproval flickers in her eyes, but she says nothing.

Michelle, either unphased by this or ignoring it, happily announces, "Marie and Butler will set up lunch soon. I will approach guests about helping in the search for Louis. Once everyone is done eating, we can establish teams."

Slowly, others filter into the dining room. Michelle jumps up with each. Some nod in agreement while others firmly decline. Jules and Camille speak with her. I'm not close enough to hear a word, but it's French anyway. A look of sheer terror crosses Jules' face, which is now drained of color. Both of his hands fly up to his head. He's pacing in place as if his anxiety is too much. Camille shoots daggers from her eyes at him. Michelle looks at me and blushes a deep red. What's going on? The situation is upsetting, but not an emergency, not yet at least. This secret—or is it secrets?—whatever it is, is big. I just don't know if it's deadly.

I busy myself with finishing my cognac and drooling over what my eyes behold making their way out of the kitchen. People begin to form a line. I join them. A green salad with vinegar and oil dressing, warm sliced beef sandwiches with provolone cheese, arugula, and tangy Dijon mustard, cold pieces of ham, beef stew, raw vegetables, slices of bread, and yellow cake with vanilla frosting. Coffee to accompany it all. While filling my plate, I marvel at my appetite.

Michelle assigns teams. Karen and I will search a portion of the vineyard while Dr. Virk and his nurse cover the remainder. Michelle and Honoré take the house and winery. Honoré whispers to Michelle in French. Her head and reply both snap at him while her eyes signal anger. My gaze turns to the interior of my coffee cup.

Dante, the fireman, enters the dining room, bumping against the doorframe, and heads for the buffet. Without a plate, he grabs a sandwich and bites into it, and mustard dribbles down his shirt. Butler moves to his side, holding a plate out. Dante sweeps it away, then takes another bite of the sandwich. Arugula escapes his mouth and drops to the floor. Dr. Virk goes to help Butler. Dante spits something in Italian to the doctor. Dr. Virk takes a step back. Recognition flashes over his face. Does the doctor understand Italian? Do they know each other? Both? Dante trips on the leg of a chair and goes down on one knee, the remains of his sandwich bouncing under the table, before pushing himself upright again. He sways in place for a moment before walking out of the room. If he's drunk again, where is he getting the liquor from? I head out to make sure he's safely up the stairs. He slips a few times, but the railing he's holding onto prevents tragedy. The slamming door assures me he's back in his room.

Karen is exiting the dining room when I turn around. "Okay, team buddy. You and I for a stroll through the vineyards. We meet back here in three hours." She looks over both shoulders. "Seriously, if we find him, I hope he's only a little hurt. I would prefer to not find him if he's . . . you know . . . *dead*."

I pull her in a tight hug and look up at the ceiling. What's wrong with our ability to choose a simple vacation?

She pushes away from me. "Let's grab coats and boots." I nod. Properly attired, we make our way to the area we're to cover. The ground isn't any better from when Honoré and I walked here. My footsteps make soggy indents that fill with water and disappear shortly after that. The smell of wet grass, grapes, and that spice I can't place.

I ask Karen if she can smell it.

"Yes, it's clover. It can smell mildly like vanilla," she replies. Once she mentions it, it's obvious. She continues, "If you're using natural insecticides, like other aggressive insects eating the destructive bugs, there must be enough food for them to stay after they've dispatched the pests you're trying to control. Clover is one source of food."

Karen stops me. "Dan, what's really going on? I know you and Honoré are gathering evidence on the accidents, but are they really?"

I drop my shoulders and release a sigh. "I don't know. Two deaths confirmed, one attempted, and one person missing. It's too much all at once. I get the feeling we're the only two that aren't holding onto a secret. Have you spoken to Michelle?"

"Yeah, but every time I do, she brushes it off and chatters about her father's birthday and how happy she is that we're here and meeting her family. Stuff like that. I can't tell if she's oblivious to what's happening or convincing herself it can't be true in her father's home. She idolizes him. That I know. She glows with pride when she talks about him. Around her I feel I'm crazy to be concerned."

"I can't get a straight answer out of Honoré. So, I'm not sure what he truly believes is going on. I know he loves Michelle and doesn't want to cause issues in the family. What are your feelings?"

"There's darkness here. I felt it the moment we arrived. The harlequin tiles that had me think of 'Masquerade' from *The Phantom of the Opera*, that led me to think of Agatha Christie's story of 'The Affair at the Victory Ball' where the character of Harlequin dies at a masquerade party. My first impression was 'death.' I'm scared, Dan."

I pull her close. I have no answers to quell her fear as I have it too. After a few minutes, she pushes back from me. "When you and Honoré were in the upstairs hall earlier, I heard you talking about getting a volunteer to try and cross the bridge. I'll do it. I know you two would be able to hold me if something goes wrong."

"No, no, no, I don't think so," I reply, shaking my head.

"It makes more sense than you doing it. I trust you and

Honoré to keep me safe. Honoré couldn't hold your weight alone. I don't have the upper body strength to help much. I don't trust anyone else here with your life."

I hold up my hands. "Give me some time to think about it. Any luck and the weather will clear enough to use phones or the internet to contact someone for help."

She reluctantly drops the subject.

We continue our arduous wander up and down the rows. Karen insists we move slowly and deliberately, eliminating any possibility that Louis was hurt and rolled somewhere obscured. Three hours later, my knees and patience have had enough. Karen agrees that he's not here.

The house feels warm as an end to the search. We remove our coats and boots. Karen shudders. "I'm gonna put on dry socks and pants."

She bounds up the stairs ahead of me. I agree with the dry clothes and make my way to our room. I step into our bedroom, and after opening the drawer that contains my socks, I'm convinced that someone has searched it. It's confirmed when I look through the other drawers. Karen emerges from the bathroom with fresh clothes on.

"Karen, were you looking for something in my dresser?"

Deep furrows appear on her forehead. "No, why?"

"I think someone was in here."

She immediately starts opening drawers where her clothes are. "You're right. I can tell because I color-code my socks and underwear. Now they're all mixed up. What could they be looking for?"

I shrug.

"Well, it's creepy," she states while getting dressed.

We meet Michelle and Honoré in the hall. Butler approaches. "Excuse me, were you able to locate Louis?"

"*Non.* I spoke with Dr. Virk and Sue. No one found him. I do not know where to look anymore or where he could be," Michelle says.

Dr. Virk appears in the doorway of the dining room. He signals for us to join him and steps back inside. Butler bows out and retreats to the kitchen. We follow the doctor. He's the only one there. The four of us form a semicircle around him. He looks around as if to be sure no one else is listening, which causes us to do the same. Content it's just the five of us, he leans in. "This may seem in poor taste, but my nurse, Sue, is retiring. Her health has deteriorated. I am sad to lose her. She's trained her replacement, so when we get back to Canada, she will not need to return to my office. I was at a medical conference in Bogotá during her last week, and I had hoped she would accompany me as my guest, but she decided she wanted to finish up at the office while it was quiet. I wanted to do something special for her for all her years of hard work. When Monsieur Bres offered this weekend to each of us, it seemed perfect." He sheepishly continues, "He paid for everything, so I asked if I could make a special dedication to her while here. He agreed. I just want to be sure everyone will come down to dinner tonight. I still have a few people to talk to."

Michelle claps her hands. "That is so nice. We all agree to be there." Karen shoots me a "what the heck" look. I raise my eyebrows and blink hard. Honoré is studying the floor.

Dr. Virk releases a long, deep breath and visibly relaxes. He smiles at us. "Thank you. See you later."

Michelle spins around. "I am very excited. It will be so nice to have something positive to do tonight. Tomorrow, we will have a big celebration for my papa's birthday."

Karen looks bewildered. "We are?"

"Yes, my papa felt that as long as he ended the murder mystery weekend because of the terrible accidents, that we would have a special French dinner with a fabulous dessert. Marie is the best French cook. Now we have this good thing tonight." Michelle has a full-beam smile on her face. I don't sense anything fake about her enthusiasm. She totally believes that everything is alright.

"For now, we should go back to our rooms to get ready for tonight. It will be so wonderful," Michelle says.

Karen grabs my hand and pulls me toward the stairs. Once in our room, she faces me. "See, that's what I mean. She's totally not dealing with the situation. I can appreciate being positive in a difficult circumstance, but this is beyond that."

"Yep, I see it. I need to speak to Honoré. We need to walk a fine line between being investigators and happy party guests. I just want to know which way he's leaning. It's important that we're never alone. I feel something's coming. I'm hoping it's something good, like Louis did make it across the bridge and headed into town for the police, but I'm not convinced of it."

"I'm gonna take a long, hot bath and try to put on my happy face," Karen says.

While she's gone, I review the reason why someone felt the need to search my room. Were they looking for something in particular? My thoughts deviate. Maybe it was to look like a search when it actually was to leave something. Quietly, I examine everything in the room. Drawers inside and out, pictures, furniture. I'm crawling along the floor, running my hand on the baseboard, when Karen's voice asks, "What are you doing?"

I place my finger to my lips, stand up, pull her into the bathroom, and turn on the faucets in the sink and tub. "Remember Honoré thought the rooms were bugged? Well, I didn't think about it until now." I explain my thinking. She agrees.

Back in the bedroom, my quest finished, exposed nothing. I think this place is getting to me. Conspiracy themes are on my brain. With my guard being up, has it led to my looking for things that aren't there? Karen writes a note for us to be more cautious with what we say moving forward. Code words: Peanut butter and jelly sandwiches indicate a private talk in the bathroom with the water running. I nod agreement. She steals a kiss and holds me tight. We need to make it out of here. Just having a plan reduces my anxiety. Karen gets it and is with me. We finish getting ready and head downstairs to the dining room.

The other guests are there, as is Monsieur Bres at a table with Jules, Camille, Michelle, and Honoré. He waves us over. Michelle is sitting on his right, happily talking with him in French. He nods occasionally in response. Honoré stares off into the distance, his face a mask of boredom mixed with agony. Jules and Camille are the same. I fist-bump his shoulder and smile. He presses a tight grin on his lips. This is going to be a long evening.

Karen leans into me and whispers, "Let's try our best to enjoy the evening."

Dinner is amazing. Chicken stew with a red wine sauce. Karen calls it *coq au vin*. I call it delicious. Cheesy potatoes in a white sauce seasoned with garlic and thyme, cucumbers in a creamy dressing with a hint of mint, an assortment of raw vegetables, warm croissants, butter, jelly, a custard tart with cherries, and mini cakes filled with sweet cream and soaked in rum. Butler is pouring glasses of a sweet white wine. Sauternes, if I had to guess.

Conversations seem light. Dr. Virk, Sue, and Thomas are seated together. Dante is absent . . . drunk? Occasionally laughter can be heard. I glance over, and Thomas appears to have relaxed some. Karen compliments Monsieur Bres on the fabulous meal. He is gracious and gives all the credit to Marie and comments on his luck of having her for so many years.

Jules stands and raises his arms. "May I have your attention, *s'il vous plaît*." All eyes turn to him. He continues, "I know this has not been the fun weekend that my papa planned. The loss of two of our fellow guests and this terrible weather. However, I hope tonight is to be a joyous occasion. Dr. Virk will address you shortly on another happy subject, but first I would like to reveal one of our winery's two newest wines." His voice catches with a muffled sob. "I am sorry our vintner, Louis, is not here to be part of this success." He sniffles back another sob and sits down.

Butler wheels in a cart with glasses filled with a dark, burgundy wine. He passes glasses to each of us. One sip and the putrid taste makes me spit it back into the glass, as does everyone.

Jules looks about wildly, completely bewildered. "Two days ago this was a full-bodied, powerful wine with a hint of cherry. I do not understand what could have happened."

Honoré makes eye contact with me. Oh, no! Please don't tell me it's full *bodied* because we just found where Louis is.

CHAPTER 13

I grab Karen by the shoulders. "Please stay here with Michelle."

Honoré and I head for the door. Thomas pushes past us, runs up the stairs, and slams his bedroom door shut. Apparently, he's freaking out again, so he won't be joining us. Dr. Virk is only steps behind us. Jules, after him, makes us a foursome. We hurry through the passageway to the vat room. Rows of tanks line both sides of the room. All resemble massive oak barrels. Each one is eight feet tall, stained a warm amber color with three wrought-iron hoops that divide the barrel into thirds. Jules points to the one he drew the dinner wine from. Honoré climbs the stainless-steel walkway that surrounds each one, releases the latch, and pulls up the top. He uses the flashlight on his phone to illuminate the inside.

"I see someone. Drain it," Honoré states.

A sudden gasp from Jules turns heads toward him. His eyes appear glassed over in fear. I move to the faucet on the side of the tank and open it fully. Deep burgundy wine flows from the spigot into the floor trap. The air smells like sweet grapes and a hint of cherries. Tension is felt as we stand there waiting for it to be emptied. Finally, the stream reduces to a trickle, then finally drops.

Honoré signals. "Dan, come help me." I join him and look inside. I've seen my share of dead bodies, but ones that have been in liquid bother me. The bloated, grotesqueness that occurs. Honoré climbs into the barrel. "I will lift him up to you." Once the victim is at a level in which I can get my arms under his, I feel wet, sticky slime that's a combination of wine and bodily fluids. I lug him over the side. Liquids run down the front of me, making a line from my chest down to my shoes. I lay him on the walkway. He's our missing vintner, Louis. Honoré climbs from the tank and joins me. His hands are wine-stained. He motions with his head to follow him to a nearby sink.

Jules steps in front of Honoré. His eyes search, imploring with Honoré until he finally asks something in French.

Honoré answers, "*Oui*."

Jules sinks to his knees, sobbing. "*Mon amour*."

Even I know that means "my love." I make eye contact with Honoré, who nods. A secret affair, or not so secret now. Does Camille know? Does she have motive? Who else does? Unfortunately, Louis will not be able to confirm or deny Jules' version of them being together during the time Honoré was locked in the garage. Whatever the reason, we have another victim. We need to get out of here or get help *soon*. Honoré is at the sink rinsing his hands, then grabs a towel and steps back, allowing me access. I finish washing my hands and dry them, mostly on Honoré's shirt as I pull him aside.

I throw up my hands without a care if anyone sees me. "What's going on?"

Honoré blushes red. "Jules is gay. He has been having an

affair with Louis. It was exposed this weekend when I confronted him about the attempt on my life."

"You didn't think to tell me? I knew you were hiding something. What else are you keeping secret?" I use finger quotes around the word "secret."

His eyes grow dark and cold. "We may be friends, but never, never presume I will do or say anything that will hurt my family."

"If *you* haven't noticed, people are dying, and they aren't accidents," I snap. "This is when good people need to show up and do what is right. You're an officer of the law. Act like one."

Honoré stands stoic, rubbing his temples. I'm so angry right now, but there's a victim who deserves the best investigation into what happened that I can give him. Jules is seated next to Louis, sobbing and rubbing his hand up and down Louis' right arm. I pat Jules on the back before kneeling beside the body and begin a basic survey of injuries. No damage to his fingernails, so he didn't try to claw his way out. It'll take a full autopsy to determine if he was dead or unconscious before being dumped in. Fingerprints on the handle of the lid will be useless as Honoré and I both touched it. Anyone could have touched it over the last day or so. The area isn't secured. I'll ask Monsieur Bres if there's CCTV footage. Maybe we'll get lucky. The vats are cold, so rigor mortis will be affected. No true time of death.

I see a set of large shoes appear out of the corner of my eye and feel a hand on my shoulder. I look up. Honoré stares down at me with his lips set in a firm, thin line. "You are right. I am a good investigator. That must come first." He puts his hand out. I grab it more as an aid to stand up, but to also affirm what he said.

"Jules, please go back to the house. Doctor, go with him," Honoré orders.

Jules shuffles off the platform as if he's sleepwalking. Dr. Virk puts an arm around Jules, steering him toward the exit.

Honoré turns to me. "Anything?"

"There looks to be a puncture mark on his neck. He may have been drugged or poisoned first, because there's no indication he tried to get out. Otherwise, nothing I can find without a pathologist."

Honoré drops his head to his chest and draws a ragged breath. "I have the key to the wine refrigerator. Let me find a cart, and we will move him." Honoré moves as if he's visibly aged since we arrived a few days ago. I'm struck by the fact of so much loss. Days only, not weeks, and yet it feels much longer. He returns with the cart. We load Louis onto it and move him to the refrigerator. He now accompanies our other victims. Something at the back of my mind is tickling a memory of a story, a book, or movie . . . I just can't get a clear image. This is when I need Karen. Her mind works differently in making tangential connections and is complementary to mine.

"Are there cameras in the winery?" I ask.

Honoré brightens up. "Yes, yes, there are. Let us go speak to my father-in-law." He heads toward the passageway with a renewed vigor. This could be the break we need. I match him stride for stride. As we step into the house, Butler meets us. "Mister Jules informed me of the tragedy. My deepest sorrows." He bows his head.

"Thank you, Butler. Where is Monsieur Bres now?" Honoré inquires.

"Working in his office, sir."

Honoré backhands my chest. "Come." He doesn't wait for me to answer but walks toward the office. At the door of the library, which is also the home office, Honoré knocks heavily.

"*Entrez*" is the response. Opening the door, warm, dry air hits me. I hadn't realized how cold the winery was. A shiver runs through me. I notice that our murder/suspect board has been placed on the floor. Honoré and I head for Monsieur Bres. He looks up at us, both stain-covered, and jumps out of his chair. "*Merde*. It is true. There was a body in the wine vat. Louis, *oui*?"

Honoré dips his head. "*Oui, Patron*. Louis."

Monsieur Bres drops back into his seat. He covers his face and mutters in low, rapid French. I look to Honoré for translation, but none comes. Again, my suspicion rises that I'm not being told everything.

I use a strong voice, "What's he saying?"

Honoré puts his hands up. "Sorry. He is upset at the death that has occurred this weekend. He feels it is his fault for inviting people here. One is a murderer." Looking back at him, Honoré asks, "*Patron*, we are interested in what the cameras in the winery may have captured."

He stares at us with a cold look in his eyes. "*Pardon*. I had them turned off."

"*Why*?" I say, louder than I intended.

He glances between Honoré and me. "It was to be a party. Clues to the murder mystery were going to be hidden throughout the property. I did not want someone to find the cameras and have an advantage in the game. I was offering one million euros to the winner." He nervously fingers his signet ring.

I rub the back of my head with my hand. I'm deflated that our best investigative tool was lost, but it's a reasonable explanation.

"*Merci*. We understand," Honoré says flatly.

I pick up the murder board as I leave. I stop at the doorway. "Is there any phone or internet connection yet?'

Monsieur Bres shakes his head.

Honoré checks his phone. "Nothing."

"If he's going to use the library as his office again, then I'll move our board to my bedroom."

We step into the hall, closing the door behind us.

"I am going to change clothes," I state. We climb the stairs in silence. Karen and Michelle are in my room when I enter.

"Is Honoré with you?" Michelle asks, looking past me.

"He's headed back to your room. We both want to shower and change," I reply.

Michelle kisses Karen on both cheeks. "*Au revoir*."

I place the board on the dresser and head for the bathroom. I strip off my clothes and step into the warm spray. I stand there, letting the water run over me. Warmed and pink-tinged, I dry off and head for the bedroom and dry clothes. Karen is staring at the board intently, her chin resting on her hands. I clear my throat, and she jumps.

"Sorry, didn't mean to scare you." I grin. "Whatcha think?"

"I feel there's a thread to all of these, but we haven't found it . . . yet. I'll ask Michelle for more note cards and markers."

I give her a brief summary of what Honoré and I found in the winery. I'm truly scared, but don't want to let on.

"I feel so sad for Michelle and her family. She and I were in the hall when Dr. Virk and Jules came up from the winery. Jules looked broken. Dr. Virk told us about what had happened. Michelle tried to comfort him, but Camille pushed her away and took Jules into the living room."

I kiss her on the top of her head and hold her close. "Jules and Louis having a relationship wasn't a twist I saw coming. I don't see a great deal of warmth from Camille towards Jules, so why go to the living room?"

Karen shrugs. "She was speaking French, so I'm not sure. I thought she said the word 'bourbon.' Maybe she's getting him a drink."

I shake my head as none of this makes sense. Karen and I decide to head down and check on Jules and Camille. At the bottom of the stairs, I hear yelling in French and follow the sound to the living room. I knock, but don't wait for a response before opening the door. Camille's face is bright red and inches from Jules'. She turns her head and focuses her eyes our way. Her anger emanates from them to such a degree that I stop abruptly. Karen places her hand on my back to stop from running into me. Jules sobs and shakes in his chair.

Camille spits out rage-filled comments in French, but I refuse to be intimidated.

I put a strained smile on my face. "Sorry to intrude, but we wanted to see how Jules was, after the shock earlier." Karen moves to stand next to me.

"Oh, he's still so sad," Karen states, ignoring Camille

and moving toward Jules. The amber liquid in the glass he holds spills some with each sob. Karen reaches out to take the glass from Jules when Camille moves to do the same. Camille grabs it; however, she bumps Karen's hand, and the glass falls to the floor.

Camille snaps, "Leave it," and begins picking up the pieces of broken glass. "Go now," she commands. Michelle enters the room, heads for her brother, helps him stand, and ushers him from the room and up the stairs. Karen and I make our way to our room. Once there, I face the murder board. "We need to add Louis. Of the people left, who would have a motive to kill him, and when was he killed?"

"I wonder if Marie would be able to give us a narrower timeframe from when he was last seen. She cooks all his meals."

"Hey, that's a good idea. I'm going to need Honoré to translate."

We see Honoré on the stairs, and he agrees that we need to narrow time of death on Louis. Marie informs us that she last saw Louis for breakfast the day before his body was discovered. Given the state of bloat, his body was in the vat twenty-four to thirty-six hours.

Honoré and I discuss continuing the investigation in the morning and make our way to bed. Karen is waiting up for me. We change and crawl into bed. I hold her tight and hope for a resolution to the situation in the morning.

CHAPTER 14

A knock at the door wakes me. Opening it, I find Thomas.

He steps inside quickly. His eyes dart around the room. "I heard Jules talking about the guy in the wine. If you still want me to try and cross the bridge, I will. I need to get out of here, and I do not want it to be in a box." His breathing is shallow and rapid.

I slap him on the back. "Let's find Honoré and get whatever equipment we can." Thomas, Karen, and I head to Honoré and Michelle's room. Once we're there, they both listen to the plan. Honoré gets to his feet and tells us he thinks he knows where we'll find rope and a harness. Our troupe follows behind as he leads us to the kitchen door for coats and boots. With everyone properly attired, he opens the back door and moves toward a large outbuilding. The skies are gray, but thankfully still no rain. Inside the building, there's an equipment room. Several bundles of rope hang on pegs on the wall, as do harnesses.

"My papa was a very good mountain climber when he was young," Michelle chirps. Honoré fits a harness on Thomas as the rest of us uncoil lengths of rope and lay it out on the floor.

"How wide would you say the gorge is?" I ask, turning to Honoré.

He crunches up his brow. "Thirty-five meters, no more than forty."

"Okay, if I do the math right, that's 125 to 130 feet. Let's measure 150 feet to be sure," I announce. At one end of the rope, I place my heel and walk heel to toe, counting as I go.

Honoré whispers to Karen, "What is he doing?"

Karen chuckles. "His foot is twelve inches long, so he's counting to at least 150 as an idea of how much rope we need."

"Ah. Does he not know that standard climbing rope is sixty meters long? I am sure that is what this is," Honoré answers.

I stop walking and stare at Honoré with an incredulous look on my face. "Now ya tell me." A belly laugh escapes Honoré, and we join him. It reduces the tension in the room.

I shake my head. "Okay, so at sixty meters, that's more than 195 feet. That should do it, but let's take more than one rope, just in case."

Karen and I wind the rope and put it on my shoulder. Our expedition heads outside and down the driveway. We slip, slide, and slush our way toward the bridge. The trip seems longer and more arduous than before. Finally, we turn the last curve when Honoré breaks into a run toward the edge, yelling, *"Non, non, NON!"*

Startled, we pursue him until we understand his reaction. The bridge is completely gone. Not a single board remains. Someone wants to make sure we don't leave or get help.

"We are trapped like animals. We are all going to die. I know it." Thomas is shaking in place, tears streaming down his face and wild fear in his eyes. Unfortunately, I agree with him, but why? More importantly, who?

Karen mutters, *"And Then There Were None.* Agatha Christie."

Yes! That's it. That's what this reminds me of. The story of invitations to a private island, no ability to escape, and death as retribution to all the guests who were determined to have committed horrible crimes and gotten away with it, until now.

Now what to do? My mind is racing, but not a lot of solutions come to me. Does anyone know we're here and to send help? Honoré and Michelle have no children looking for them. Karen and I are sure that our son, Eric, will be concerned that we haven't checked in for a few days, but doubt he'll be able to locate us. The last he knew, we were in Paris meeting old friends and would talk later. What about the other guests? Would anyone have a family member or friend that would miss them enough *and* know our exact location?

Honoré is rubbing his forehead. Is he trying to comprehend what's going on? Karen places her hand on my arm. I hug her tight and say, "We'll be okay."

"Dan, you understand that in Christie's novel everyone dies at the end." Her eyes reflect a mixture of fear and sadness.

"Shhh. Peanut butter and jelly sandwiches," I reply. She nods acknowledgement.

"Sandwiches? You are thinking about food at a time like this? What is wrong with you? We are going to die! You heard her. Do you understand?" Thomas shouts, then places his hands over his face, crying into them.

"Michelle, you said that your father bought a helicopter and it's here, right?" Karen inquires.

"*Oui*, but there is not a pilot here, and my papa has not yet started his lessons to learn to fly it," Michelle says.

A sly grin creases Karen's face. "But it should have a radio we can use to contact help."

I kiss her all over her face. I knew she was brilliant. Thomas and Honoré are already scrambling up the driveway. I grab Karen's hand and she grabs Michelle's as we follow suit. Each of us slides, falls, and crawls up the mud-encased road. Slowly we find our way closer and closer to the house. Thomas bursts through the kitchen door, which bangs loudly against an interior wall, then the rest of us push in, unfortunately frightening Marie. She is pressed against the refrigerator, holding a large meat cleaver with a look of terror on her face. Michelle maneuvers her way to stand in front of her, speaking French in a low, soothing voice. Gradually, Marie releases her clenched arm, lowering the knife. Michelle continues speaking to her until Marie's face relaxes and she points with the cleaver to an area beyond us, down a narrow hallway.

Michelle smiles at Marie, then turns to us and announces, "She said the keys to the helicopter are on a pegboard in the hall." Really? I know I do that with my car keys, but this is a bit more expensive machine. The entire crew spins around and moves like a comedy routine down the hall. Five adults were never meant to fit in it. Shoulders bumping, groaning, and nearly tripping play out until we face the pegboard. *No keys.* Honoré rests his head against the wall with his eyes closed.

Michelle gently pats Honoré's arm. She happily says, "I will ask my papa if he has the keys with him." Our band of characters follows her to the library. We stand in the hall. She knocks and waits. Nothing. She opens the door, peers in, and looks around. "He is not there. He may be upstairs, napping." Butler suddenly appears behind us and confirms that Monsieur Bres has retired to his private quarters but will be down later in the afternoon.

"I am *not* running around this place. It is too dangerous. I will wait in my room," Thomas says, looking around wildly. He dashes up the stairs and slams his bedroom door.

Honoré puts his hands up. "I will check the helicopter to see if there is a way to get to the radio. The rest of you can all stay here."

I don't want to sound distrustful of Honoré, but I am, and plan to go with him just to be sure of what's happening. "I'll go as backup." I force a laugh. Honoré shoots me a look but doesn't protest.

Karen and Michelle head to the kitchen for something warm to drink. Honoré and I walk to the helicopter. I'm just happy to see it's still here. It sits on the remains of a concrete floor from a building that was removed. It's a Robinson R44 model. Beautiful. I walk around it, appreciate the simplistic elegance of this machine, stare inside, and may even drool a bit. Honoré pulls on the pilot's door. Locked. He moves to the passenger's side. The same. He pulls out a credit card. "This works in the movies." He maneuvers it back and forth, then up and down while pulling on the door handle. A crisp snap reveals that he broke off part of the credit card in the door. I'm not sure which of us is more shocked and disappointed, but I can't completely repress a laugh.

"Well, this is not a movie, just a nightmare," he states

flatly. "When you are done laughing, maybe you will have a good idea."

"Besides trying to break through the glass on this, I got nothing. Still no phone reception?"

He pulls his phone out, holds it up, and walks in a serpentine pattern. "No. Not one bar anywhere." He releases a deep sigh.

"Let's head back and check with your father-in-law to see if he has the keys and any ideas."

The trek to the house is done in silence. We find Michelle and Karen sitting at a long kitchen counter with cups of hot tea, munching on chocolate cookies. I lean on the granite countertop; its coldness permeates my clothes, and I pull my arm up. Michelle gets up and fills a cup each for Honoré and me. The warm liquid slides down my throat, and I emit an involuntary shutter.

"Anything?" Karen asks.

"No, the helicopter was locked up. We need to talk with your father, Michelle, about finding the keys and if he knows if anyone here is a pilot," I say.

"My papa will gladly help," Michelle chirps with a smile. She's really not getting the seriousness of the situation. Marie steps back from what she is stirring in a pot on the stove. It smells wonderful. Subtle herbs infuse butter. She opens the oven and brushes warm rolls with the butter mixture. She snaps something in French.

Michelle jumps up. "Marie would like us out of *her* kitchen." Michelle grabs our mugs and puts them in the sink, even if we aren't finished. Oh well. She directs us toward the hallway, where Monsieur Bres is exiting the elevator. He kisses Michelle on both cheeks. She says something in French.

He replies, "*Oui*, in my office." He steps forward, leading us to the office. He swings the door open. Sue Jannsen, Dr. Virk's nurse, jumps and quickly closes the center drawer of the desk.

"What are you doing?" Monsieur Bres demands in a loud baritone voice.

"I . . . I . . . I lost an earring last night and was hoping someone found it. I wanted to speak to you, monsieur." She stops, making eye contact with him, then shakily continues, "But as there was no one here, I thought I would look for it, in case you have what I was looking for."

Monsieur Bres' dark eyes grow black. "In my desk? Nothing is in *there* that would interest *you*." A devilish grin sits on his lips.

"Of . . . of course not. I'm sorry. I meant no disrespect. I'll just go." Her voice trails off at the end. She gives a feeble wave. "See you all later. Oh, if anyone sees an earring, it's probably mine. Thank you for everything." She quickly leaves the office, her eyes downcast. What the heck was that? I get the feeling there was some subtext going on between her and Monsieur Bres. What would she really be looking for to be so desperate to search his office? Karen squeezes my hand. We'll talk later.

Monsieur Bres opens the recently searched drawer. "I have a set of keys here." He pushes documents around the interior. He removes several sheets of paper and continues to feel inside the drawer, then looks up. "They are not here."

Honoré runs his hand through his hair. "Well, as the office and, apparently, your desk are not locked, anyone could have removed them at any time. *Patron*, the bridge is completely gone. We are looking for a way to get help. Are you aware of anyone here that could fly the helicopter?"

He shakes his head slowly. *"Non."*

"Do you know everyone well enough to be sure?" I jump in.

"I am not aware that anyone is a pilot," he snaps.

Undeterred, I push more. "What about the phones or the internet? Are they working?"

He checks his computer and phone and says they're not working. I don't trust how honest he's being or has been, so I will be asking guests if they have the skill to fly a helicopter. If the internet were working, I'd review a video, but then again how hard could it be to fly one? I just need to make it a few miles over the gorge. Up a little, left, then land. Definitely a solid Plan B.

CHAPTER 15

Honoré and I step into the hall. He turns to me. "Come."

My eyebrows knit together with curiosity and concern. "Okay, where are we going?"

"Breaking and entering a helicopter. I have had enough," he snaps in reply, stomping toward the kitchen. Shock leaves me in place for a second or two. Long enough that Honoré is gone. I move through the kitchen. The open back door indicates his path. I proceed out onto the driveway as Honoré flings open the side entrance to the garage. Brave to return to the scene of the crime or pissed beyond caring? My suspicions of Honoré nag at me. I stick my head in cautiously. He's digging through the drawers and boxes on a workbench.

"What are you looking for?"

His eyes flash red with anger. "A hammer, an axe, anything big and heavy enough to smash the window of the chopper. I am getting to that radio. Ah!" He pulls out a hammer and shows me.

"That'll work."

He thrusts his thumb in the general direction of the helicopter and stalks out of the garage. I'm on his heels. Moments later, we're standing next to the bird. Honoré is next to the passenger-side window and rears the hammer back above his head when I yell, "*Stop!*" He nearly hits himself in the head as he pulls the tool back. "What?"

"It's gone." I point to a now-empty space in the console.

He lets the hammer fall to the ground, presses his face closer, and spits out, "*Merde.*" We both step closer. There is a gaping hole where the radio should be. Torn wires dangle like spaghetti strands. Whoever took it did so in a hurry and without thought of returning it. We stand there, our mouths hanging open. Disbelief, fear, and anger surge through me as it must also for Honoré.

"We were not gone that long. Who could have even known what we were doing?" he throws out rhetorically. "Thomas. He ran off. He *must* be the one behind this. I will beat him until he tells me where that radio is." Honoré charges toward the house. I do my best to keep up with him. We reach the house simultaneously.

I grab his shoulders. "Stop. We need to think this through. Let's approach Thomas, but please, no violence." Honoré is puffing in short breaths and glares at me.

As calm as possible, I continue, "We're trained interrogators. You know as well as I do that getting angry at the suspect shifts the power. We lose objectivity. We're better than this." I search his face for recognition.

He closes his eyes, leans against the wall, and begins a rhythmical nod. His breathing slows as he releases a series of deep sighs in succession. "*Oui.*" He places a hand on my arm. "We can go question Thomas." I turn toward the stairs when I hear him mutter, "If talking does not work, then I will beat him." I roll my eyes, but don't comment.

Our footsteps echo in the empty hall as we ascend the marble staircase. A chill runs through me as I realize it feels cold and eerily quiet. Honoré takes the lead and knocks, or rather bangs, on Thomas' bedroom door. Nothing. He repeats and calls out to him. Still nothing. He tries the door, and it opens with a creak. Why hasn't he barricaded himself in? No, no, no, please no more death. Honoré pushes the door open further, calls out to Thomas, and steps inside. It's empty, and I mean empty. All of his things are gone. The closet is open and barren. I check the bathroom. No toiletries or any personal items. He's disappeared, but to where, and is it of his own volition? Honoré taps me. I shrug. "I have no idea. Where would he go, and how?"

Honoré takes a sharp breath and runs out of the room. I spin on my heels to follow, but not sure why. He traverses through the house, then steps outside and toward the helicopter. Once it's in sight, he stops short. I can't stop in time and bump into him. He glares down at me. Yeah, one helicopter, still missing its radio. Standing there, he drums his fingertips on his lips, thinking. I wait for him to share. He snaps his fingers and runs back toward the house. He heads for the shed that holds the climbing gear. I'm a fair piece behind. He bangs through the door with so much force that it snaps back into his face, hitting his nose. No blood, but he's doubled over, holding his nose. "*Merde,*" he snaps, then stands upright. We stride across the doorframe. All the climbing gear is missing. I push past Honoré.

"What the heck?" I say more to myself, trying to fathom the scene. I spin around and around to be sure that I'm not missing something.

"He could try to escape down the north face of this mountain. It is a sheer drop, but there is a chance with a harness and enough rope. An experienced climber, or a lucky one, may be able to make it. My question is this, is he escaping because of what he has done here, or to access help for us?"

We head for the area Thomas would have tried to scale down. Climbing rope is secured, thrown over the side of the cliff, and disappears out of sight due to the angle of the rocks.

Honoré creeps closer to the edge. A wave of anxiety rises in me. I can't breathe, my muscles are rigid, and images of Honoré slipping and falling off the edge make me want to scream "*Stop!*" at him. Honoré walks back toward me, and a strong sense of relief washes over me.

Honoré twists his lips to one side, looks back at the edge of the cliff, then back at me. "He might have tried to climb down, or this could be just a red fish."

"Uh . . . ?"

"You know, it is not what is. It is just something to confuse us."

"You mean a red herring?"

Honoré sighs in frustration. "That is what I said. Maybe he escaped, maybe he too is dead here or somewhere else. I don't know what to believe even when I see it."

Suddenly, I'm drained. Exhaustion doesn't even begin to describe my feelings. Physically, mentally, emotionally. I'm one setback away from either weeping or laughing in hysteria. I need Karen. She is my center. I want to hold her close, know she's safe, and breathe. Honoré trudges back to the house. My legs feel weighed down, but staying in place isn't an option.

Before I know it, I'm in our room, and Karen is there. She approaches me, throwing her arms around me without saying a word. We stand there, lost in time, until she asks, "What's going on?"

I recap everything since leaving Monsieur Bres' office. She sits on the end of the bed. I can see the wheels turning in her mind. She tilts her head from side to side as if weighing options.

"What?" I ask hesitantly.

Karen begins pacing. "Well, in the Christie novel *And Then There Were None*, the murderer was someone who faked his death, which left everyone remaining to suspect each other. No one thinks a victim is the killer."

I rub my fingers over my chin. "Thomas may not be dead. It's a ruse to avert suspicion away from him."

"Was there evidence that he actually scaled down the mountainside?"

"No. Rope was thrown over the edge. Honoré said he didn't have a clear view down to the ground."

"In the book, the mastermind was free to kill at will because no one wanted to check on a corpse," Karen states. "Which is true for someone thought to have escaped, if we stop looking for Thomas."

"The grounds need to be searched again. If Thomas is our killer, I need to find where he's hiding," I say as I step for the door.

Karen is right behind me. I turn to question her as to what she's up to.

"Not 'I,' but rather 'we' need to search," she answers.

"No," I say, shaking my head. "I want you to be safe."

"And I want *you* to be safe. We're here together. Good or bad. I'm done sitting here, scared that you're hurt or worse, hoping you come back."

A quiet groan escapes me. This is not in my plan.

"Can you say that you trust Honoré a hundred percent? If not, then I'm your backup." Karen stands her ground, her eyes unwavering in their determination.

I release a sigh. "Fine. Where was the murderer hiding in the book?"

"Each victim was put in their assigned room with the door closed, so he hung out in his room between murders."

I nod and head for Thomas' room. We enter with caution. If he is our killer, this would spoil his plan. The room is as Honoré and I left it. Empty. "Not a creature is stirring, not even a mouse." A low chuckle follows. "Where to?"

"The rooms of the other victims?" Karen suggests.

We check Corey Ander's and Bill Ding's. Disappointed. Nothing is different from when Honoré and I closed them.

As we step back into the hall, Honoré is there. His arms are crossed over his chest, and his head is cocked to one side. "What are you doing?"

"Testing a theory," I reply.

"Any you care to share with *me*?" he asks with a tight smile on his lips.

Karen chimes in, "Well, I had this silly notion that it was like in a book. Dan was kind enough to humor me, but I was wrong. Nothing to report." She shrugs nonchalantly.

Honoré's eyes flick between us as if evaluating the validity of Karen's statement. I roll my eyes. His face relaxes. "I will see you later." He turns on his heels and heads back to his room.

Once back in our room, Karen and I head for the bathroom and turn on all the faucets.

"That was awkward," I mutter.

"I wish I could be sure that he's to be trusted. In the book, the murderer has an accomplice in staging his death, until the killer turns on the accomplice. So, is Honoré a good guy or not?" Karen says.

I shrug in response. "The grounds still need to be searched. Louis had a room too. It's out of the way with little pedestrian traffic," I state.

"We'll need to ask Marie if she's noticed food gone missing. If Thomas didn't plan to hide food prior, he'll need to sneak in and eat."

A remote dinner gong resounds from downstairs.

Karen slaps my knee. "Come on, let's get ready and try to enjoy the evening. I wonder if Dr. Virk is still doing his thing to say thank-you to Sue? Maybe a good glass of wine will help us relax."

An involuntary shudder runs through me at the memory of the last glass of wine I had.

"Sorry, okay, maybe not wine." Karen forces a laugh.

We dress and head toward the stairs. Dr. Virk emerges from his room and follows us down. As we enter the dining room, Butler hands each of us a glass of sparkling wine. I accept one with trepidation. Karen and I join Honoré, Michelle, Jules, and Camille at the table.

Monsieur Bres sits with Dr. Virk, Sue, and surprisingly, Dante, who may be sober at this moment as he appears showered and dressed appropriately.

Michelle looks between me and Karen. "I feel I need to apologize. I have been made aware . . ." She shoots a sideways glance at Honoré, who is studying his glass, then continues, ". . . that I have been annoyingly too happy. What is the word you Americans use?"

"I think the word you're looking for is 'chipper,'" Karen remarks.

"*Oui*, 'chipper.' I wanted you and my family to have happy memories of this weekend, but that will not be true," Michelle says.

Karen reaches out and grabs Michelle's hand. "What's important moving forward is finding solutions to how to get help and keep everyone safe."

Honoré cuts in. "Dan, I think we will search the grounds. Thomas may still be here but hiding."

I don my best poker face. "Really? You think he's our killer?"

"I do not know that. What I do know is that I need to do something. I was thinking about what Karen said about this being like a book. Thomas could want us to think he escaped. Maybe he is now hiding. Searching needs to happen."

"Okay. That's a plan. In the morning after breakfast, we'll start."

Michelle says, "Karen and I will keep a list of where you have searched and make sure no place was missed."

"Um, I'd like to go with Dan. Maybe you could go with

Honoré," Karen suggests. She turns to Camille. "Would you be willing to keep the list? It would really help us."

Camille says, "I do not want to be a part of this. I am afraid."

"We all are. Helping would give you something to do, and hopefully this will be resolved soon," Karen retorts abruptly.

Camille nods but doesn't look up from the table.

Jules snaps, "What about me?"

Honoré stutters, "Ah . . . you could ask Dr. Virk to make a team, then we will cover more places."

Jules sets his jaw but doesn't reply. An awkward silence descends on the table until Butler announces that dinner is served.

CHAPTER 16

A plate filled with roasted chicken, warm bread, sauteed root vegetables, and quiche lorraine eases some of my anxiety. Curious, no dessert tonight. Karen sips her wine. "Yum, this is great. Sweet, not too dry. I can drink this."

I stifle an involuntary gag as I watch her. "Have mine too." I pass the glass to her.

Honoré is tucking into his food with gusto. No guilty conscience? Jules pushes his food around the plate. Camille fires an angry look at him. Michelle and Karen are discussing books. As I eavesdrop, it's apparent that Michelle is well versed in the Agatha Christie novels, their plot twists and endings. She's talking about the fact that she had just finished reading *And Then There Were None*, which gave her the idea to suggest a murder mystery weekend. *What?* I hadn't suspected Michelle up to now. Was that a mistake on my part? She'd have intimate knowledge of the buildings and grounds, but her personality never presented itself as having a dark side. Christie liked having the least expected person be the killer. Wheels are turning in my head. Looking back, I wonder if there were times I should have suspected. Would she have wanted Honoré dead? Or could that have been someone else? One killer . . . two . . .

more? Is this more like the movie *Strangers on a Train?* You do a murder for me, and I'll do a murder for you. That way each has a firm alibi. It doesn't feel like it fits. Then who, and why these people, and why now?

A utensil clinking on a glass brings me out of my thoughts. It's Monsieur Bres. All eyes turn to him. "*Messieurs* and *mesdames*, your attention, please. I beg your indulgence. I would like there to be some level of celebration tonight. I ask that you allow my esteemed physician a few minutes of your time. Doctor?"

Doctor Virk stands and coughs to clear his throat. "Thank you, Monsieur Bres. I have been a doctor for a long time and owe a great deal of my success to the nurse who worked beside me for much of it, Sue Jannsen. I have a small token of my appreciation. It is not nearly enough for all your hard work and dedication. Please come up here."

Sue looks around as if he's speaking to someone else. She makes eye contact with me. I can't tell if that's surprise or fear. She walks to Dr. Virk, who opens a gray velveteen-covered box, pulls out a diamond-encrusted, heart-shaped locket, and unfastens it. Sue turns her back to him. He drops the necklace over her head, allowing it to rest just above her breasts, and closes it at the back of her neck.

"Ouch," she mutters, raising her hand to her neck.

Concern spreads across Dr. Virk's face. "Did I hurt you?"

"Just a scratch," she replies.

"Oh, it's bleeding. Could I have a small bandage, please?" he asks, looking around the room.

Butler steps from the room only to reappear moments later

with a bandage. He hands it to Dr. Virk, who opens it and places it over the cut. "There. Hope that is better."

Sue places her hand over the locket. "Thank you for this." She gazes up at the doctor with a pressed smile on her lips.

"I could not have done it without you," he says.

"And I know where the bodies are buried," she retorts. Audible gasps can be heard in the room. *Really?* She thought that was the best response? Sue's face flushes deep red. An uncomfortable look crosses Dr. Virk's face as he struggles for something to say. Monsieur Bres holds up his glass. "A toast to Sue on her retirement."

"To Sue" comes a group response. We raise our glasses and take a drink. Nice save, Monsieur Bres.

The lights dim suddenly. A wave of uneasiness takes hold of me. Tensions rise throughout my body. What's going on? I allow my eyes to adjust to the low light and survey the room for any and all threats. Monsieur Bres catches my eye. He grins. Can he read my body language and knows this situation sets me on edge?

Butler opens the door for Marie, who carries in a flaming dessert. Cheers erupt as she places it in front of Sue and presents her with a knife. Butler lays a stack of small plates and forks next to Sue. He returns to again turn up the lights. Sue quietly claps and blows out the flame. Applause punctuates the room. Butler portions out slices and delivers them to each guest. I feel myself release the breath I was holding and roll my neck to release the tightness in it. Karen digs into her dessert. "Ummm, this is amazing." Butler moves through the room with a carafe of coffee. Together, they finish off another wonderful meal.

A loud pop from outside causes everyone to jump. I duck in case that pop is someone with a gun entering the room.

Monsieur Bres announces, "Nothing to worry about. Those are the fireworks I ordered for my birthday, but this is a better celebration. Everyone, please step outside to enjoy them."

"How wonderful!" Michelle exclaims. Still chipper. Oh well.

We head into the hall for our jackets and file out the front door. Standing on the driveway, looking up as the colors light up the night sky, it's a peculiar mix of comfort and apprehension. Fireworks invoke memories of joy, summer fun, and being carefree, but here there's an air of foreboding that I can't shake. Karen leans into me; I feel her warmth. She whispers, "I'm feeling the effects of the wine." "Ohhs" and "ahhs" are heard. The finale is deafening and resounds in my chest. I feel compelled to do a head count. All present, accounted for, and more importantly still alive. A procession files back into the front hall. Butler gathers the jackets from each of us. Dr. Virk says his good night and heads upstairs.

Sue says, "I feel a headache coming on. Maybe I had too much wine. Thank you everyone for a lovely evening."

Monsieur Bres bows to us as he ambles toward the elevator. Camille stomps up the stairs without any acknowledgement to us. Jules traipses behind her.

Honoré taps my shoulder. "Come, *mon ami*. Michelle and I would like you and Karen to come to the kitchen. Let us sit and talk like friends, not investigators."

Dante pushes past us with a partially filled bottle of wine in each hand and playfully dances upstairs. I can guess what he plans for the rest of the evening.

The kitchen feels warm and inviting as the scents of dinner linger in the air. We sit on stools around the center island. Michelle is surveying the contents of the refrigerator. A pot of coffee, leftover rolls with butter, and cherry tarts are too much for me to resist.

"Michelle, please thank your father for the fireworks. It was so much fun to see them," Karen states.

"I will. It was to mark the end of the weekend with a winner of the game named and the money awarded. I am sad that we are stuck here. I feel I ruined your vacation." Tears well up in her eyes.

"Don't cry, because then I'll start to cry. No one should cry alone," Karen says.

Honoré looks at me with a questioning look as if to say, "What happened?"

I've got no response as I'm not sure either.

"No one should be crying now," Honoré snaps, glaring at Michelle. She sniffles. So much for talking like friends.

Honoré grunts, "Let us talk about tomorrow. We can hope for clear skies and the ability to call for help. We can meet at breakfast and set up a search grid."

"Sounds good."

Honoré reaches over and takes Michelle's hand, squeezes it, and gives it a shake while speaking in a low, soothing tone in French. "I'm sorry I snapped at you" looks the same in any language.

Michelle smiles weakly. He drops her hand, then turns to me. "Did you find anything interesting in William Wright's room?"

"Who?" I ask.

"Bill Ding, remember?"

I scoff out loud. "I forgot they had real names. My mind has been so messed up by everything that's happened so far." I'm avoiding the direct question.

He doesn't relent. "Find anything?"

"No. It's actually as we left it. Fingerprint dust and all. Nothing's been disturbed."

"Did you check Corey Ander's? Drew Taylor?" His gaze is intense and focused on me.

"Yeah," I reply.

"Why did you feel the need to look?" Honoré questions.

Karen jumps in. "Well, that was me. I love mystery stories, and in one, a supposed victim was a killer. He faked his own death and preyed upon the other guests because no one suspected him. But this isn't like a book. Dan was really kind to show me that."

Honoré's eyes narrow as he processes Karen's explanation. "Did you bother to ask to look in the winery refrigerator? I have the key." He pulls it out of his pocket to show us.

"No, that would have been the easiest thing, but I liked being a part of the investigation, even for a little while," Karen says in an uncharacteristically little girl tone.

"Well, to put your mind at ease, we will go to the winery and check the refrigerator." He pushes his stool back and abruptly stands up. His face is an unreadable mask. Is he truly interested, wanting to be helpful, or calling us out on our explanation?

As Karen stands up, she stumbles and uses the countertop to steady herself.

"You okay?" I ask.

"Wow, that wine went right to my head. I have the start of a headache. I didn't think I drank that much," she answers.

I look her in the eyes. "Do you want to go back to the room?"

"I must insist that we check the winery first!" His voice is more an order than a request. My "coppy senses" are now on alert. I'm about to object when Michelle cuts in. "Karen, I know Marie keeps aspirin or something for pain here. I will get it."

Karen sits back on the stool as Michelle throws open cabinet doors and drawers until she pulls a bottle out. "Ahh. Here."

She shakes two pills out into her hand and motions for Karen to take them. I silently will Karen to decline the pills. I hate being paranoid, but as of this moment, I trust Karen and myself *only*.

"That's very kind of you, but I've had bad reactions from some medications in the past. My doctor gave me strict orders to only take the medication he's prescribed for my headaches. I have some in my room." Karen gives Michelle an effortless smile. Michelle shrugs and pours the pills back into the bottle.

"Shall we?" Honoré indicates toward the door, still wiggling the refrigerator key.

I look at Karen, who nods. My mind is racing. If this is a setup, what weapons do I have at my disposal? Honoré leads the way out of the kitchen. Michelle is behind him. I take Karen's hand and pull her so she walks behind me. I'm a human shield. We continue down the hall leading to the winery. I take an inventory if there are items on the walls in the event I need to fight our way out. Nothing. The walls are bare. While walking, I feel Karen slip something into my hand. It's cold and sharp. *A knife.* She must have taken it from the kitchen before we left. I love my warrior woman wife. I slide it into my back pocket and squeeze her hand to acknowledge it.

Honoré looks back over his shoulder. I focus straight ahead, my pulse pounding. This is a fatal funnel. Enclosed on both sides, poorly lit, moving to an open area that could have an ambush waiting. I feel my stomach tighten with each step. My breaths are shallow and ragged. Entering the vat room, Honoré proceeds to the door of the refrigerator and unlocks it. Michelle moves to the right of it. I stop at the end of the tunnel and visually inspect every inch of the room. Karen is still behind me. I release her hand. I'll need both if it comes to a fight.

Honoré swings the oversized door open. "Dan, what are you waiting for? Come here and see."

I step forward only as far as the opening, keeping Honoré in front of me. He pulls back the sheets covering the victims, one by one. "See, this is Bill Ding, and Louis Moreau, and this is . . . *What the . . . Where is . . .*?"

The last sheet covers cases of wine. Honoré proceeds to spin around as if he'll see what is missing. "*Non . . . non . . .*"

Confusion replaces my anxiety. "Where's Corey Ander's body?" I snap.

"I do not know" is Honoré's angry response. "It was here. We both saw him. *We* put him in here, together." He continues to search for the third body, shoving cartons of wine out of the way, peeking behind shelves. I don't think Corey rolled behind them on his own. Honoré puffs in frustration with each item he moves. He pulls a crowbar off the wall.

"What are you doing?" I ask.

"I will open every crate," he replies tersely.

"Unless someone cut him, and only him, into pieces, he won't be found in a wine box. They're twelve inches all the way around, at most," I throw back at him.

A noisy clang resounds as he lets the crowbar drop to the floor. His face reflects his attempt to pull forward a reasonable explanation for why the body is gone and what to do next.

"Are you sure he was dead?" Michelle asks quietly.

Honoré's eyes blaze at her. "Dr. Virk swore he was dead!"

"Oh . . . no" is a quiet utterance from Karen. All eyes turn to her.

She continues, "In the book, the doctor was the accomplice to the killer. The doctor verified the victim was dead when he wasn't. Right before the doctor was killed." Karen grimaces.

A loud foot stomp causes us to turn toward Michelle. She does it again while shaking her fists at us. "Stop saying that. This is not a book. This is my papa's home. These were terrible accidents. No one is killing people here." She covers her face as she weeps uncontrollably. Honoré pulls her close to him, speaking quietly to her in French while stroking her hair. Karen and I stand by silently. Minutes pass until Michelle sniffles, steps back from Honoré, and wipes both eyes with the palm of her hand. He and I make eye contact.

"It is late. We can deal with this in the morning. Let us go back to the house," he states.

Honoré and Michelle shuffle toward the hall leading to the house. Even though my tension level is lower, I still want them in front of me and Karen behind me. This is how we walk to the kitchen. Honoré and Michelle continue toward the hall without hesitation.

Karen stops. I turn to her. She leans her head into my chest, sighs, and mumbles.

"Pardon?" I question, lifting her head so I can see her lips.

"I said, 'What is wrong with us?' We took a knife to follow our *friends*. I feel scared all the time. I'm reading a double meaning into everything, and they're all dark."

I run my hand through my hair. "Yeah. It's this place. I want to believe Honoré and Michelle are good people, but I don't want to be naïve either. Let's try and get some sleep."

"We should check on the doctor," she says as we walk in the direction of the stairs. "But you're keeping the knife, right?"

"Absolutely," I state. "And you should have one too."

She winks. "Already do."

CHAPTER 17

We make our way up the stairs, then stop at the doctor's door. I knock. Nothing. Knock again. Still nothing. Karen looks at me, anxiety in her eyes. I'm reaching for the doorknob when the door pulls open.

"What?" Dr. Virk's eyes are mere slits as he tries to focus on us and negotiate the increased light in the hall. A lock of hair has fallen over his forehead, and he's wearing a light-blue pajama top and pants. They resemble hospital scrubs.

"I . . . umm . . . I . . . a . . ." I fumble for an explanation as to why we're there that doesn't sound totally crazy. "Just checking to be sure you're alright."

"I was fine until you woke me up. Go away," he replies, slamming the door closed.

"Now I sound like an idiot," I tell Karen.

"Well, I'd rather annoy him than find him dead," Karen declares.

"True, but I'm ready for bed. How about you?"

"Me too. I just can't shake this headache," she replies.

In our room, I slide the bolt lock in place and wedge a chair under the door handle. It's like a movie scene from the 1950s. I'm not sure it will deter anyone, but any advance notice of an intruder is a good thing. We change quickly and fall into bed. Mine is a restless sleep. Every noise convinces me someone is trying to enter our room. Several times during the night, I check on the security of the door. I'm suddenly aware of another sound. It takes a moment to fully comprehend what it is . . . rain. Not a soft drizzle but the heavy, driving storm that started this adventure four days ago. Dread washes over me. This eliminates any chance that the phone or internet signal will return.

Karen rolls over. "What time is it?"

"6:30."

She scans the room in bewilderment. The reality dawns on her. She looks at me. "It's pouring outside again, isn't it?"

"Yeah."

She lies back against the pillows. "Are we ever gonna get a break? I just want to get out of here."

I nuzzle in close to her, feel her warmth, and inhale the lingering scent of her perfume. She wraps her arms around me. Maybe we'll stay in this room until help arrives. Moments pass until she pats my back. "We need to start the day, like it or not, and try to find a way out of here," she states flatly.

I roll out of bed and make my way to the shower. The water revives me. Dried off and dressed, I step into the bedroom. "I'll wait for you while you get ready. We stick together from now on."

She lets out a deep sigh, pushes herself to a standing position, gathers her clothes, and heads into the bathroom. Cold, gray drops hit the window. I will it to stop, but to no avail. The weather gods are not listening to my pleas. Karen exits the bath and joins me. She snarls at the window. A low snort escapes my lips.

"Ready?" she asks.

The air in the dining room is filled with the smell of coffee, which aids in my revival. Eggs, sausages, a roll, and fresh fruit along with a cup of hot, black coffee. Karen opts for a more continental breakfast. Dr. Virk enters the room and glares in our direction. Camille and Jules walk in behind the doctor but avoid any eye contact. They situate themselves as far away from us as physically possible. I'm enjoying a second cup of coffee when Honoré and Michelle join us. They notice that we have finished eating and ask that we stay and sit with them. Not like I have a lot of other places to go today.

"I hope you slept well. I did not. I could not stop thinking about what had happened. Maybe today we will find some answers," Honoré says.

They fill their plates. While they eat, we discuss the return of the terrible weather.

Karen fidgets in her chair.

"You okay?" I ask.

"Well, Sue didn't come down. I'm worried. Can we check on her?"

I open my mouth to reply when Sue walks in. She's pale and wearing sunglasses.

Karen approaches her, and the two converse. Sue heads to where Dr. Virk is sitting. Karen makes up a plate of food and a cup of coffee, which she takes to Sue, who accepts the coffee but waves off the food. I'm suspicious. I doubt she's that hungover. Is something else the cause of her not feeling well?

Karen leans close to Sue's ear and says something. Sue takes a bite of a roll and washes it down with coffee. Karen rubs Sue's shoulders, then returns to our table.

"Is she alright?" Michelle inquires hesitantly.

Karen nods. "Horrible migraine. She was only going to have coffee, but I convinced her to also try and eat something, especially if she's taking medication. Dr. Virk thinks he may have something that might help if she's not feeling better later."

"We're only missing Dante," I state.

Honoré guffaws. "That is not a surprise. He is sleeping off his latest bender. He will be down when he is hungry, or more likely, *thirsty*." He taps his finger on the table. "We will plan to search the buildings and grounds today. First, I will talk to Dr. Virk about Corey Ander." He stands up abruptly and strides over to the doctor. Dr. Virk's head snaps up as Honoré is talking, nodding vigorously. Honoré slaps the doctor on the shoulder and returns to our table.

"He has no explanation for why the body is not there. He is certain that he was dead," Honoré relates.

This makes no sense. Why move the body, and who moved it? It serves no useful purpose that I can think of. If he wasn't really dead, then is he behind the other deaths? If he was dead, does someone want us chasing phantoms, but why? To buy time? To do what? A voice brings me out of my thoughts.

"Dan, Karen, I have decided we will use the living room as our new office as it seems my father-in-law is using his. We can move all the information we have to date there. Meet us in twenty minutes," Honoré says emphatically.

"Will do," I say as it wasn't so much a question as a directive. I take Karen's elbow as we head for the hall. Butler stands in our way and whispers, "Might I ask you a question, sir?"

I look around me, curious as to its nature and the hushed tone. "Sure."

"Marie has brought to my attention that sometime last night, one of the guests seems to have taken several bottles of wine, one of which she needs for a recipe today. I am inquiring as to whom that may have been."

My thoughts go immediately to Dante and his carrying bottles upstairs last night, but I'm not comfortable with implicating anyone. "Offhand, I can't think of who that would be. I'm sorry."

Butler bows slightly. "Thank you for your time, sir, madame." He steps aside, then turns back. "Sir, Marie is also sure that two knives are also missing. Would you know anything about those?"

I shrug and shake my head.

"Again, sorry to bother you," he says and moves toward Dr. Virk. Karen and I make our way to our room.

As the door closes, Karen turns to me. "What was that about?"

"I'm not sure, but I'm not about to start naming names."

We take turns brushing our teeth and prepare to meet Honoré in the living room. Karen reaches for the doorknob when there is a knock down the hall. She pulls her hand back as if the knob might bite. I step past her, open the door, and investigate the hallway. Butler is knocking on Dante's door. Someone gave him up. Butler's knocking gets more insistent, to no avail. I'm sure that Dante is sleeping off his latest binge. Good luck waking him. Karen and I start to descend the stairs when I hear Butler. "Sir. *Sir!*"

I turn on my heels and run toward his voice. He's standing in the doorway of Dante's room, door open. His eyes are transfixed into the room. What does he see?

"What is it?" I ask.

He doesn't answer. He's frozen until I grab his arm and break the trance. Terror is on his face. I can't tell at first what he's looking at until my eyes adjust to the low light. I step further into the room. Karen is at the door saying something, but I'm not listening because at the same time, I notice not what, but who. Dante's head hangs off the side of the bed, his eyes and mouth gaping open. I step forward and feel for a pulse on his neck. Nothing. He's cold to the touch. I back out to the doorframe, explain the scene to Karen, and ask that she find Honoré.

I move Butler to a chair in the hall. He sits down. I kneel in front of him. "Why were you up here?"

"It is terrible . . . just terrible. How could . . . was he drunk? What could have happened? I must inform the master. What do I say?"

I grab his shoulders and force him to look at me. "Why were you up here?"

"I-I-I was checking on the missing wine. I-I-I just needed to ask him. He did not answer, so I . . ." He drops his head into his hands, muttering. After a moment, he shakes himself and draws in a deep breath. "This will never do. The master must know." He pulls himself up, standing very straight, regaining his composure. "Excuse me, sir." Then he turns and walks toward the elevator.

Honoré bounds up the stairs, Karen and Michelle behind him, in that order. "What is wrong?"

I motion with my head in the direction of Dante's room. "He's dead."

Honoré exhales dramatically. "How?"

"I haven't done anything other than check for a pulse. You have your phone? We'll need pictures of the scene."

Honoré closes his eyes and leans his head back. I give him a few minutes until finally, "*Honoré!*"

His eyes focus on me. "I know. Again we need to do this."

A faint whimper escapes Michelle. Sadness floods her eyes. I feel bad that this horrible drama continues. I flick my gaze to Karen, who places her arm around Michelle and directs her back down the stairs. She'll take care of her while Honoré and I process yet another death.

"Honoré, do you still have any supplies in your crime scene kit?"

"Not much," he replies with a hefty sigh. "I did not conserve what I had after the first scene. This is our fourth investigation. I did not think I would be doing this repeatedly. Let me check what I have."

"I'll use your phone and mine for photos now. Once we fingerprint the light switch, we can turn the lights on and see what's happened," I say with a total lack of enthusiasm.

Honoré heads for his bedroom. Standing alone in the room, I inventory the scene. The door wasn't bolted from the inside, so either Dante didn't remember to lock it, wasn't concerned for his safety and didn't feel the need to, or was too drunk to care.

Honoré returns, places the kit down in the hallway, opens it, and surveys the contents.

"I have some dust and strips to lift a few prints. We need to make conscious decisions on what to process," he states.

"We'll do the light switch first. After that, we can turn the lights on and decide from there," I say.

Honoré moves to the light switch, dusts it, and lifts some prints. "What about the door handle?"

I shake my head. "Butler has already touched it, so I'm not sure we'll find anything useful."

Honoré concurs. He flips on the lights. Both of us stop and stare, shocked by what we see. Dante's exposed extremities are a bright cherry red.

"*Merde*," utters Honoré. I can't say it better myself.

"This makes no sense. His color is the significant sign of death by carbon monoxide poisoning. Is the heat in each room on a separate furnace?" I turn to Honoré.

"I would not think so, but that is a question for my father-in-law."

"There's no other explanation unless he was killed in the garage and moved to this room. It's crazy to think someone would do that. Let's start taking pictures."

Honoré hands me his phone. I move around the room, snapping pictures from every angle. When I'm done, Honoré dusts and lifts prints from the empty bottles at the bedside, the thermostat, and Dante himself for elimination as he refused to provide them in an earlier part of the investigation. I bag and tag the wine bottles. Honoré places paper bags over the victim's hands. A discreet cough from the doorway draws our attention. Butler is there with Monsieur Bres and the cart. Monsieur Bres steps into the room and begins speaking rapidly in French. Honoré blushes pink and replies in French.

My ire is up. "What are you two talking about?"

Monsieur Bres shoots an evil sideways look at me and lowers his voice but continues in French. He dramatically pokes Honoré in the chest with his index finger. Honoré clenches his hands shut tight and opens his mouth to reply when his father-in-law snaps at him, turns on his heels, and leaves the room.

I check my anger, knitting my eyebrows together to try and convey more confusion than suspicion. I need Honoré to keep me informed on what is said.

Honoré drops his head to his chest, flexes his fists open and closed, and breathes slow and deep.

"You okay?" I ask.

"*Oui*. He is just a difficult man to deal with. He wants me to *figure out* what is happening to his guests and catch who is doing this. He said that the heat is on a central unit, so it is impossible for one room to have a malfunction. He also insisted that his daughter be protected."

Butler steps into the room, pulling the cart as he does. It contains a folded sheet. I take more photos before we lift Dante onto it and cover him. Honoré, Butler, and I proceed solemnly to the elevator and then to the winery refrigerator.

I make sure both are in front of me, the knife in my back pocket. Honoré unlocks the door to the refrigerator and swings it open. He and Butler place Dante's body on the floor. Corey

Ander's body is still absent. I move only as far as the door-frame. Butler exits the refrigerator with the cart. I take steps backward as Honoré slams the door closed and locks it. He returns the key to his pocket.

"You are sure *he* was dead?" comes his question.

"Yeah, he was cold to the touch and rigor mortis had set in. He's been dead a number of hours. There's no faking that," I state. "I know you have a key. Where did you get it, and who else has one?"

He tilts his head to one side. "This is Louis'. I'm sure my father-in-law has one unless the keys are hung on the wall in the kitchen like all the others."

I snap, "We need to find out."

CHAPTER 18

We trudge our way from the winery to the kitchen and find Marie poised at the stove, stirring the contents of a pot. The smell of beef broth hangs in the air. Honoré asks her about keys for the wine refrigerator. Both speak in rapid and animated French. My head swivels between them like a verbal tennis match until Marie stops talking and turns her back to Honoré.

Honoré motions for me to follow him into the hall. "Marie says there are three sets of keys. My father-in-law, my brother-in-law, and Louis. I have his. We need to find Jules and ask if he has his key."

"What about speaking to your father-in-law?" I ask.

Honoré waves me off. "Not now."

"Why not now?" I refuse to break eye contact with him. The sound of footsteps descending the stairs draws our attention. It's Jules.

Honoré meets him at the bottom, grabs his elbow, and propels him into the dining room. I follow them but can't understand the French.

Honoré stands with his feet planted and arms crossed over his chest. Jules bows his head. His body begins to quiver.

Honoré rolls his eyes and throws up his hands. Jules sobs as he retrieves the key from his pocket and shows it to us.

"He did not move the body. He can't stand to see his lover's body in that situation."

Honoré turns toward the hall. I step in front of him. "So now we need to speak to Monsieur Bres."

"*Non!*" Honoré explodes. "He is upset that his daughter and guests are being hurt and angry with me because I have not solved these accidents."

I push my face closer to Honoré's. "Because they're not *accidents*, they're *murders*."

We glare at each other for a few moments. I'm not about to back down. Honoré blinks first, then steps back and releases a deep breath. "*Oui*, they are," he says quietly.

I check my emotions. "We need to investigate, no matter what."

Honoré nods. "We will, I promise. First, we must search to eliminate any other possible suspects." He walks into the living room, which he's requisitioned as our "incident room." I'm trying my best to contain my anger.

Karen, Michelle, and Dr. Virk are already in the room. Jules joins us, having regained his composure. A map of the grounds is laid out on the coffee table. Honoré assigns areas to be searched. Teams are established. Honoré and Michelle are one team, Dr. Virk and Jules another, and finally Karen and I. Michelle says that she wanted Camille to help but she begged off, reporting a headache. Jules avoids all eye contact at the mention of Camille.

Karen asks Dr. Virk about Sue's migraine. He states that

he gave her some medication and she's sleeping but should be able to make dinner tonight.

Raincoats, boots, and flashlights are provided. Jules and Dr. Virk leave to check the garage and outer buildings. Karen and I have the winery and vineyards. Karen and Michelle quietly talk to each other as Honoré heads for the hall. He snaps something in French to Michelle, never breaking stride. Michelle blushes and scurries after him. Karen rolls her eyes at me as she'd never let that behavior slide without comment.

Once in the winery, I look at Karen. "This is crap!"

"What?" she asks, bewildered.

"Honoré's reluctance to confront his father-in-law about this situation. Monsieur Bres is the common denominator to all the people here. He needs to be questioned about everything and everyone!"

"I tried to approach Michelle about the same subject, but she again defended her father and said he doesn't know anything and he's upset by what's happening."

I run my hand through my hair. "Well, I'm gonna ask him. Honoré can come with me or not, but I'm beyond caring what he thinks."

Karen lays her hand on my arm. "I appreciate what you're saying, but maybe more questioning and less confronting would be a better approach."

"I'm a skilled interviewer when I choose to be." I shoot her a sideways glance and grin.

"That you are, my love." She laughs out loud. "For now, let's do our due diligence and search our assigned areas. When we get back to the house, we'll include Honoré and Michelle in the plan. If they hesitate, you know what you have to do, and I'll support your actions."

The search takes longer than I expect, but Karen and I inspect everything to no avail. Nothing is out of place from previous searches. No one has been here since. Louis' room is still a horrendous mess. I can't understand living in that, but it doesn't affect the investigation. Outside in the vineyards, the cold and wet seep into us, and we are more than happy to return to the house. We go to our room and change into dry clothes.

Honoré and Michelle are in the living room when Karen and I arrive. They report that they found nothing different. We update them when Jules and Dr. Virk return. They too found nothing.

"What's next?" I ask, staring at Honoré.

He averts his gaze and focuses on the carpet. I wait for his response. Nothing comes. My patience ended, I open my mouth when he makes eye contact with me and snaps his head in the direction of the hall. "Come."

"Where are we going?" I inquire.

"To speak to my father-in-law. It is time he answers some questions." He stomps to the door and steps into the hall. I agree that it's overdue. I grab a notebook and pen prior to leaving the living room.

Michelle runs after him. "I will come too and speak with my papa."

Honoré turns on his heels and harshly says, "*Non.* No more. I am investigating multiple deaths. No more family interference."

Her expression couldn't have reflected more hurt or sadness if he'd slapped her in the face. I feel a pang of guilt at the pain this is causing her, but this needs to happen.

Honoré strides to the office, opens the door, and looks in. He shakes his head, so Monsieur Bres isn't there. I follow him to the elevator. He pushes the button.

"How are we playing this?" I ask.

"Huh?"

"Am I playing good cop? Or I could be bad cop, if it helps."

He knits his eyebrows together. "I will be direct with him. No good or bad cops here."

That's disappointing. I'd be a good bad cop.

"Okay," I answer, stepping into the elevator with him.

The ride up is quiet and awkward. Even the elevator feels slow as it moves toward the top. My anxiety rises. I'm uncertain of Bres' reaction to being questioned. We exit on the third floor, and Honoré positions himself squarely in front of the apartment door. He raises his hand to knock but pulls it back. My mind wills him to knock. A shudder runs through him. He releases a deep, cleansing breath, shakes his whole body, stands bolt upright, and knocks with authority.

"*Entrez*" comes the reply.

Honoré turns the knob and swings the door open for us to enter. The room is eerily dark. *"Come into my parlor,"* says *the spider to the fly.* Slivers of light creep in where the curtains meet. Monsieur Bres is seated in an upholstered chair against the wall in the far corner of the room. An easily defendable position. Does he actually think like a cop? I can respect that.

Honoré clears his throat and croaks out a barely audible

"*Patron*, excuse the intrusion, but we have some questions for you regarding what you know about each of your guests." I guess he left his confidence at the door.

A slight head incline from Monsieur Bres is his only response. My anxiety is creeping up the scale at a steady rate. My eyes, now adjusted to the low light, dart around the room in a serious threat assessment. The exit is behind me, and I'm going to keep it that way. No one else is in the room. Is Monsieur Bres armed? Would he want us both dead if we uncover any secrets?

"*Oui?*" Monsieur Bres questions.

"*Patron*, can you give us information on the guests here this weekend?" Honoré's voice is a whisper. Well, he's not about to ask any hard-hitting questions. This cements my decision to ask them.

Monsieur Bres begins to reply in French. I'm done being left out of conversations, information, gossip, or any other verbal exchange between the two of them.

"*English!* I'm here to investigate and learn the truth as well." I glare at Monsieur Bres. I don't flinch, I don't even blink.

Honoré puts his hands out to calm me, or us. "No need to be harsh, Dan. Please understand." Honoré presses a grin to his lips.

I hold back the anger I want to unleash on them both. I need to be more spider and less fly now. I hear the door open behind me. I turn to see Michelle and Karen in the doorway.

I persist. "No! These deaths happened on our watch. Anything he or anyone can tell us could hold the key to everything. No matter how insignificant it may be. Will you help us?"

Monsieur Bres' gaze flicks to Michelle, then me. He smirks, but there's an intensity in his eyes. I believe he realizes I played him into a corner and have beaten him at his own game of being large and in-charge. He relents. "Yes, I want to help."

Michelle pushes past me to embrace her father, kissing his forehead and smiling. In battle, use any weapon available. Michelle's love and belief in her father is the one thing he's defenseless against.

Karen is at my back, exactly where I want her. Near the exit, alert to any danger for us both.

"What do you need to know?" he asks.

Honoré gushes with relief. "Thank you. See, Dan, he wants to help us."

"Yes, I see." I lock eyes with Monsieur Bres, and we each know that's not the truth of the situation. A little less willingness and much more coercion, but at this point, I'll take anything. No matter how it's obtained.

"Um, well, I guess, um . . ." Honoré stumbles over his words as if he were a rookie cop.

I've never been shy at interviewing anyone. "We'll need background information on each victim. Where they're from, possible enemies, anything you think would be helpful," I assert. No grin, unwavering eye contact, and feet planted as if I've taken root.

"We need to continue this in my office. There you may ask what you want. Give me thirty minutes. I want to have my lunch," Monsieur Bres states flatly. Michelle stands next to her father, rubbing his shoulder. I've never had the impression this man needs emotional support. My eyes catch movement to my right. A panel slides open. Butler steps into the room and places a tray in front of Monsieur Bres.

Secret passage? It unnerves me to realize my defense plan of keeping the exit to my back and having an unobstructed view of the room is a fallacy. I shoot a glance at Monsieur Bres. His expression assures me that he knows that I know he's still the master. If he does help us, it's because *he* wants to.

Honoré stands and says, "Thank you. Thirty minutes or as much time as you want. No hurry. We will have lunch as well." He slaps me on the back as if this has settled all my concerns.

"What, no, we need to get some answers," I say.

"We will, Dan. Not to worry." Honoré tries to sound assuring.

I roll my eyes. Michelle kisses the top of her father's head and coos something in French. Michelle, Honoré, Karen, and I take the elevator back to the ground floor.

Honoré gleefully heads for the dining room while holding Michelle's hand.

I look at Karen as if I've missed something. She shrugs and gives me a "whatever that was" look. She takes my hand and leads me to the dining room.

Honoré opens the door. I look over his shoulder. Dr. Virk and Camille are huddled close together. They quickly step apart, then Dr. Virk takes a seat at a far table. We sit down, and Camille joins us. Guilty of something?

"Camille, how's your headache?" Karen asks.

Confusion flashes on her face. "My what?" Realization dawns on her. "Oh, *oui*, better. *Merci*."

"Will Jules join us for lunch?" Michelle asks.

Her eyes narrow and darken. "*Non*."

Awkward silence hangs in the room until Butler enters with a cart filled with food. Hopefully not the same cart we transport the victims on. He places a platter of sandwiches, a bowl of soup, fresh fruit, and an apple tart on the buffet. "Lunch is served."

We each fill a plate and return to the table. Camille takes hers and leaves the dining room. Curiouser and curiouser. Sue passes her in the doorway. Camille practically pushes her out of the way. Sue appears startled but recovers and comes to our table.

"Thank you so much for helping me," Sue says to Karen. Sue has better color in her face, and she's lost the sunglasses.

"Headache is gone?" Karen questions.

"Most of it. It's a lot better. Thank you again." Sue turns toward the buffet and takes a sandwich.

"I'm glad she's better. It took a while for my headache to subside. She seemed so much worse than me, so I was hoping that Dr. Virk would be able to help her. It looks like he did," Karen comments.

Michelle and Honoré mutter agreement. We finish lunch. I'm anxious to get started interviewing Monsieur Bres. Before Honoré and I head for the office, Karen lets me know that she and Michelle are headed to the living room to reorganize the evidence board. I kiss her head and hug her tight. She hugs me back.

"Stay safe," she whispers in my ear.

"You too," I reply.

CHAPTER 19

In the office, Monsieur Bres is seated at his oversized desk. He motions for Honoré and me to sit in the low chairs in front of it. From our perches, we must look up at him. Power and control. I'm willing to let Honoré take the lead right up until he doesn't, then I'll jump in.

"What would you like to know?" Monsieur Bres asks pleasantly.

Honoré coughs. "Umm, your guests. What do you know about them?"

His father-in-law presses his fingertips together and narrows his eyes until all I see is darkness that fills them. "What I'm about to say must go no further. I am a man of business. Keeping secrets on how I practice is a large part of my success." His eyes soften, and he smiles. "And my daughter's uncompromising love for me is my greatest treasure. I cannot lose that." His gaze shifts between Honoré and me.

"I believe you. She is a special woman," Honoré gushes.

Really? I may have just barfed in my mouth. I can't believe Honoré is playing into Monsieur Bres' script. I keep it to myself.

"Absolutely," I reply and nod. During an investigation,

I'm allowed to lie to suspects. He tops my list, so yes, I'll lie in the hopes he'll just confess to it all and give us why right here and now.

Bres removes a manila file off the top of a stack of such files. He lays it in front of him, opens it up, and skims the contents. "Drew Taylor, a.k.a. Corey Ander, was a brilliant chef. He won nearly every prestigious award possible. He was the 'golden boy' when he opened his first restaurant. However, as with all things, newer and younger chefs came behind him. One bested Drew, who could not handle it. He started a campaign against the young chef."

"What do you mean by a 'campaign against the young chef'?" I ask.

A sly grin creases his lips. "Drew began a crusade of sabotage, including paying people to post bad reviews of the chef's restaurant, making calls to the health inspector, and bribing staff to plant damning evidence of health violations when inspectors toured. The young chef suffered devastating losses. Drew's behaviors were eventually exposed. He lost everything."

I can't control myself, blurting out, "*Why* would you have him here?"

Confusion washes over Monsieur Bres' face, who incredulously responds, "He is an amazing chef. His food is legendary."

"But you must admit what he did to the young chef was terrible," Honoré asserts.

"Oh, yes. True," Monsieur Bres concedes.

I shake my head in disbelief. "Anyone here hold a grudge against Drew?"

"No one I know of," he responds with only the slightest tilt of his head. He rubs his signet ring. Could that be his tell when not being truthful? Is there more to the backstory or the reason Drew was here?

"What can you tell us about Bill Ding?" Honoré inquires.

Monsieur Bres opens another file. "Bill Ding's real name was William Wright. He worked as a building engineer, but he was better at design than construction. He allowed substandard materials in a building. It collapsed partway through construction, killing six men."

"Why was he here?" Honoré looks at his father-in-law with dismay.

"He comes cheap. Desperate men do." Short and to the point. "He needed the work, and I needed an engineer on a project I am starting. He was here, in part, to discuss the plans. It seemed easiest to have him come for the weekend."

I lean forward in my chair. "What is the project?"

Monsieur Bres waves a dismissive hand at me. "*That* is unimportant to your investigation."

Honoré agrees enthusiastically. "That is true. Dan, we do not need to know that." I stare at Honoré and open my mouth to say something, but before I can, he's asking questions. "Any possible enemies here this weekend?"

"*No!* We don't know what facts of the project are important or not until you tell us what it is. A family member may have issues with William's designing another building after one of his killed six people," I retort.

His father-in-law shakes his head and spins the ring. "A hospice facility here in France."

"A worthy cause. I doubt anyone would have an issue with that," Honoré chimes in.

Of course, noble, and I can't prove if it's the truth.

Honoré continues, "Do you have background on Louis, the vintner?"

Anger flashes in Bres' eyes, and he places his fingertips to his mouth before responding in a metered voice, "He came highly recommended. Words like 'innovative' and 'ahead of his time' were used to describe him. He seemed to be the man to grow my winery business."

Time to poke him, hoping in anger he'll reveal something. "And his relationship with Jules? What were your feelings on that?"

Monsieur Bres glares at me and juts his head forward. "He crossed a line. My son was not homosexual until him."

It worked! No time to stop. "Jules reports otherwise. He called Louis his 'love.'" I emphasize the "love" with finger quotes.

A low growl emanates from Monsieur Bres. Anticipating an outburst, I reflexively lean forward. Seconds tick by as he stares at the carpet. When he makes eye contact with me, he has regained his composure and waves in a vague manner. "We French are passionate and use the word 'love' freely. There can be experimentation without commitment."

So much for my ability to bait him into a confession.

Honoré mutters incoherently, "True, true. Then there is Thomas Thomas."

A smug look upon his face, Monsieur Bres replies, "He is the son of an old friend. Thomas' father's firm was my plumber of choice on many of my projects. When he passed, I was asked to look after his son, to make sure he succeeds. I have watched his progress from afar. This weekend was a good excuse to see him again after many years. I am worried as to where he could be." His gaze flicks to me. I don my poker face, but don't believe his sentiment.

"Any reason to think he could be our killer? Does he know the victims?" Honoré asks.

"I do not believe he is the killer or that he knows the people here" comes the reply.

"Would you happen to have any information on Dante Fuoco, the man we knew as Les Burn?" I ask.

Monsieur Bres snorts in disgust.

"And?" I push.

He looks at me sideways with his mouth open, as if he can't understand why I want to know, until he relents. "The man was a fool and a drunk at the end. I am not surprised he died young."

I knit my eyebrows together. "Then why invite him?"

"Because he was once brilliant and saved me millions."

Honoré looks between us. "What does that mean?"

"I had a failing business that conveniently burned down. Dante worked some magic, and the proposed arson ultimately was listed as an electrical fire. Insurance covered my losses and more," he states dramatically and smiles to the heavens.

Repulsion surges through me, my brain on fire as I rise halfway out of my seat. "You sanctioned arson and a cover-up?"

Angry, demonic green eyes flash during his reply. "I did nothing. The business manager did. The death is on him."

Bile in my throat gags my next question. "What death?"

"Unfortunately, the business accountant was working late and was unable to escape the flames. It was a terrible consequence." Monsieur Bres relaxes and leans back in his chair. His eyes challenge me to lose my temper.

I open and close my fists in an attempt to calm myself, searching for what to say or ask next, until I'm interrupted by Honoré's statement.

"Well, you cannot be held responsible for the situation if your business manager did it without your knowledge." His voice drops to be barely heard. "It was without your knowledge, correct?"

Monsieur Bres snaps an affirmative nod.

"Then you have no blame in it," Honoré gushes.

What? There have been times in my career when my frustration has pushed me to consider reaching over and shaking a suspect. This would be one of those times. However, I'm torn between who to shake, Monsieur Bres or Honoré. Wildly, my brain searches for a competent line of questioning when I'm suddenly aware of my role versus my position here. This isn't just about me as an investigator. Karen is also here, and in how much danger?

"We're looking at everyone remaining as a suspect. Are you aware of anyone with a motive?" I ask.

"I know all the guests here except *you* and your wife." There's a pause for effect before he continues, "There is no reason to want any of these people here dead. Could there be someone else we know nothing about?"

Distrust creeps into my voice. "You want us to believe that

an unknown killer just happened to be here this weekend? I'm positive that is not what we have going on."

Monsieur Bres throws open his hands and shrugs.

"Dan, my father-in-law would never hurt his guests. We are still investigating people remaining." Honoré lets a nervous laugh escape. "I do not believe Dan or Karen are murderers, are you?" He turns to me, a thin smile on his lips. Wrong time for levity.

"You can never tell about a person," I snap more vehemently than I mean to. Mentally I tell myself to play along with the charade and be less confrontational. "But if it isn't us, that leaves Dr. Virk, Sue, Butler, Jules, or Camille, unless we think it could be Marie."

Laughter erupts from Honoré. "I vote for Marie."

Monsieur Bres shoots a deadly look at Honoré while mumbling something that sounded like "Stupid." Uncomfortable silence follows. Honoré either ignores the comment or he didn't actually hear it, but he presses on. "Seriously, *Patron*, what do you know about Dr. Virk and Sue?"

"I trust them fully. Both are dedicated healers. I am living proof of that. I cannot see why they would want to hurt anyone."

My anxiety is climbing. This is useless. I know he's not telling us everything he knows. Honoré is going along with wanting to think the best of his father-in-law, and Monsieur Bres is eluding us with every answer.

"Jules works for you and knows these people, and then there's Camille. What about either of them having a motive?" I ask.

Honoré's head snaps to look at me, his mouth ajar. Monsieur Bres drops his head in resignation. "I admit my son is not the businessman I had hoped he would be. He does not use his head. I fear leaving the company I spent my whole life building, but I am old. It is time." His voice lowers. "Camille is too simple to even think about hurting anyone. She believes in butterflies and rainbows."

That's not the impression I have of her.

I lean forward and push my forearms against the edge of the desk. "Mr. Butler. What's his backstory? Is that even his real name?"

A smirk crosses his face as he replies, "Of course! His backstory, as you say, is he is a professionally trained English butler. Highly regarded in his field. He should be for what I pay. He was working at a business associate's home when I decided that he would bring a certain polish to my household, especially as I'm often not here to be involved in the day-to-day running of the house. He is a wonderful member of my staff."

He's given us nothing to work with. No suspects, no motives, and no direction to push the investigation toward. Rolling around his statements in my brain only raises my frustration. Honoré is never going to push for him to be honest. My neck tightens, and I feel pain at the base of my head. Tension headache building. What to do next? Who to question? Butler is definitely on *my* list.

A phrase pops into my thoughts, '*Softly, softly, catchee monkey,*' which makes me smile. I don't need a confession, at least not today. I'm not going anywhere, and neither is he.

There's no statute of limitation on murder. The evidence and victims are here. Tension releases from my upper back and shoulders that allows me to recline in my chair.

Confusion replaces anger and confidence on Monsieur Bres' face at my relinquished attitude and smile. I like that he's off-balance. If Monsieur Bres is our murderer, I can play the long game. I stand and extend my hand to Monsieur Bres. He unwillingly shakes it. Honoré follows as I step out of the office and into the hall.

CHAPTER 20

Once in the hall, I turn on my heels. "What is wrong with you?"

"I do not understand what you are talking about," Honoré replies.

"In there." I point my finger to the office. "And this whole weekend. You've acted more afraid of your father-in-law than of being a good investigator. People are dead, so I repeat, what's wrong with you?" I realize my face is mere inches from his. His next statement slaps me hard.

"I am."

"Huh?"

"Come." He motions with his head toward the front door. Completely bewildered, I follow him.

He steps outside onto the driveway. "You must tell no one."

Silently, I nod agreement.

"I am afraid of losing Michelle."

"You mean if you convict her father, she'll leave you?" I ask.

"No. Well, maybe. When her mother died and her father seemed to be lost, Michelle's grief was so deep she did not care about anything. She stopped eating or sleeping. She cried all the time. I tried and tried to make her happy, but nothing worked. I had the priest come and talk, but it didn't help." Tears run down this bear of a man's face. I feel terrible for bringing up those memories.

He breathes in a shaky breath. "Then her father got better. He lost weight, started eating better and working out, and seemed to be happier. He talked about giving the company to Jules to run. My Michelle got better too. She laughed and smiled again. She loves that old man with all her big heart."

He places his hand on my shoulder. "I am afraid, my friend. I do not want to believe he is involved, but if he is, it will break Michelle. I do not know what to do."

I close my eyes and tilt my head back. There is no good answer here. What would I do if this situation were Karen and me? Ethically, it's wrong not to investigate fully.

"Honoré, we will gather the evidence. When the local authorities arrive, they can do with it what they want. No judgment from us on a suspect. Agreed?"

"I can live with that." He throws out a big hand, which I shake. We make our way back inside.

Michelle and Karen are setting up the revised murder board as Honoré and I enter the living room. Note cards of different colors indicate established categories. Suspects appear to be anyone still in the house. Our known victims are also there. Thomas Thomas and Corey Ander's cards are on the desktop. I wrestle with the idea of presuming they're dead. Both could be, or only one.

"How was Papa? Helpful, yes?" Michelle asks. Honoré nods enthusiastically. Karen faces me and understands I have a different take on the subject but says nothing. I'm running scenarios in my head about the next step. Karen pats my arm.

Honoré examines the board. "That is very good. I see you have all the necessary information."

Michelle happily talks about Karen's ability to organize the information into a useful tool.

Honoré strolls to the coffee table where the intact bottles of alcohol were placed after the liquor cabinet fell on Bill Ding. He begins to make cocktails. He adds gin and several other liquids before topping them off with champagne. I'm ready for a drink, but not a celebration. When he has four glasses, he distributes them. One sip, and I look at him.

He smirks. "French 75. Classic cocktail. I may need a few more of these the way this investigation is going." Michelle puts her glass down and heads out of the room. Karen and I ding glasses. Michelle reappears shortly with a tray of sliced cheeses, nuts, and fruit.

"These are just leftovers, but they are still delicious," she offers. We settle into the couches, sip, and nibble in quiet.

Honoré points to the board. "Karen, have you discovered anything Dan and I missed?"

While she finishes chewing, she shakes her head, takes a sip, then says, "No . . . but I have the feeling something's there. I'm just not sure what, if that makes sense?"

Honoré runs his hands through his hair and releases an exasperated sigh.

"Karen, if you had to guess, what do you think the 'something' might be? A person?" I question.

"Ummm, I'm not sure. It's a puzzle that when put together will form a pattern, but everything's a jumbled mess, as if someone's moved colors from one row of a rainbow and put them somewhere else," she replies speculatively. "I just need more time to put it together." Time is one thing we don't have.

"Can we walk through each situation?" Karen inquires. "I'll write down which of the guests and staff were in the area when it happened, what led up to the moments, and if any of the suspects have an alibi."

We agree it could be helpful.

"Honoré, please start with Corey Ander, a.k.a. Drew Taylor," I state.

He scans the board. "Okay, Drew was a chef who had been unkind to a young chef in the past, was here to cook the birthday dinner, and was found alone in his room from what we think were poisoned candies. What am I missing?"

"Besides his body?" Michelle snickers, then points out that we can't be sure he's even dead. She adds, "He had a nut allergy that he mentioned to everyone."

"Butler," I blurt out. They all turn to look at me. "Butler was knocking on Drew's door. That's what caught my attention. He was holding a cup of hot cocoa that he said Drew requested and that he had knocked but hadn't tried the door. We don't know that's the truth. He could have easily handed the tainted sweets to Drew, then stepped out and waited for Drew to die."

Karen writes down Butler on a card and places it in the suspect column.

"Can we fingerprint the box the chocolates were in?" Michelle asks, leaning forward.

"The authorities would be able to. However, if he did deliver a box to everyone, then his fingerprints will be on all the boxes," Honoré answers.

I close my eyes and picture the scene. "Also, Dr. Virk picked up the box to move it when he examined the body. So his prints will be on it."

My turn. "Bill Ding, a.k.a. William Wright. He was an engineer with a shady construction past that caused six people to die as a result of negligence. Monsieur Bres asked him here to be part of a new project. His clue for the murder mystery brought him into this room to check the liquor cabinet that, when opened, pulled away from the wall and crushed him. Sue, Dr. Virk's nurse, was with him, and her screaming alerted me. Karen and I were in the hall. Who else was there?"

Honoré involuntarily shivers. "I think I was trapped in the garage at that time."

"Oh, sorry," I say. I look at Karen.

Karen closes her eyes. "Give me a sec to think. Our first riddle sent us to the office. We found our second one, came back into the hall, passed Honoré. Dr. Virk was coming in the front door because he said that was where his first clue led him. Butler was there and I think perturbed that Dr. Virk was dripping on the hall floor after being outside in the rain."

"Where did Butler come from?" I ask.

"I'm not sure. He was suddenly behind me, then went to assist the doctor with his wet coat. The problem is that both crimes weren't random and could have been set up in advance. The chocolate poisoned and left in the room to be eaten whenever and the liquor cabinet positioned to fall when opened. The trick would be to ensure who opened it," Karen says.

Tapping his fingers together, Honoré remembers, "We had wine with dinner that night. No one made a cocktail. The cabinet could have been set hours before the start of the murder mystery game."

Karen mutters to herself, then repeats it out loud. "It's not a trick. Butler was giving out the clues that night. He could have easily made sure who received which clue." The color drains from her face as she looks at Honoré. Acknowledgement flashes through his eyes. He was meant to get the clue that caused him to be in the garage.

Oblivious to the realization, Michelle adds, "The same is true for Louis. Jules said he was with him for the last time during the second night of the game and arrived back in the house after the cabinet fell. We do not know when he was killed and placed in the wine vat."

I rub my forehead, coaxing my memory. "Then there's Les Burn, I mean Dante Fuoco. We saw him heading to his room the night he died, but didn't see anyone enter or exit the room until his body was discovered . . . wait, until Butler again got my attention by knocking on Dante's door, then alerting me."

Karen scribbles Butler's name again and places it on the board.

"But how do you simulate carbon monoxide poisoning but not affect anyone else's room?" Honoré questions.

"My guess would be a small gas stove placed in the room and left running without ventilation," I answer. "But there wasn't one in the room when we went in. If there was one, who brought it in, and how? I doubt anyone would risk being seen dragging it in and out through the hall."

Karen tilts her head to one side. The wheels in her mind are working, but on what?

Honoré begins to pace, muttering softly to himself in French.

Michelle sips her drink. "These murders seem very personal. It is a shame."

We all turn to look at her. She's unphased by the remark. I open my mouth to say something, but snap it shut. Duh, isn't all murder personal, especially to the victim? I close my eyes to think of a solution to overcome the screaming in my head that's repeating "Michelle is clueless."

Karen's hand on my arm brings me out of my thoughts. "That's the piece of the puzzle. They're personal." She smiles at me. I roll my eyes. She's spent too much time with Michelle. She smacks my chest with the back of her hand and repeats, "They're *personal*."

She points to the board one by one. "Drew, the chef, dies of suspected food poisoning; William, the engineer and builder, has a cabinet fall on him and crush him to death; Louis, the vintner, drowns in a wine vat; and Dante, the firefighter, dies of carbon monoxide poisoning.

I grab her in my arms, kissing her all over her face. "Genius. I married a genius. These murders were very *premeditated*. Someone is seeking revenge."

"Who?" Honoré is looking between Karen and me.

We both shrug.

"But if Thomas fell off the cliff trying to escape, that does not fit. He is a plumber," Michelle adds.

"He may not have been murdered. If he was trying to escape and fell over the edge or was pushed, it could just be an accident, or the murderer needed to improvise as Thomas wasn't following the plan."

"That much planning would narrow our list of suspects to anyone with the knowledge of who is attending, like . . ." Honoré's voice trails off. He avoids all eye contact.

"Like my papa! *Non!* Butler also knew," Michelle snaps, her eyes ablaze with anger.

"Why would Butler know?" I ask incredulously.

"He is Papa's secretary too. He handles everything in the house and any correspondence. He planned the whole weekend. Papa is too busy."

The hall gong sounds. Honoré and Michelle head upstairs to get ready for dinner. I wouldn't want to be him behind closed doors. Karen stands and I take her hand, but in the hall pull her toward the office. I look inside. Empty. We enter.

She whispers, "What are we doing?"

"Covert mission. I want to look through the files Monsieur Bres has on everyone without him having the opportunity to censor what he tells me. Watch the door."

The files from earlier are no longer on the desktop. I pull drawers. Locked. I shift my weight from foot to foot, deciding if I'm willing to do some breaking and entering. I am! Taking the letter opener off the desk, I push it into the lock and jiggle it until it releases. I yank open the drawer, pull out a stack of manila folders, and shuffle through them to find Butler's. I look over both shoulders just to be sure, then skim the contents. Most of it is basic background information: name, date of birth, education, and previous employers. My eyes widen at what I read next. Motive and opportunity. I have it. Quietly I return everything to the drawer, close it, and wipe down any surface I may have touched. I motion for Karen to head for the door. We step into the hall. No one there. We make our way upstairs. At the top, I stop abruptly. Karen bumps into my shoulder.

"What's wrong?" she asks.

I point in measured beats to Dante's door. How does one simulate carbon monoxide poisoning without being seen? If Monsieur Bres' room has a secret door, do others? I have to know and make my way to Dante's room.

Karen is on my heels. "Dan, we're gonna be late for dinner."

"Five minutes," I reply. She gives me that "I've heard that before" look.

"Okay, six minutes, tops. I promise."

I step into Dante's room. Karen follows and closes the door. She throws up her hands and furrows her brow. I mouth, "Secret passage." She rolls her eyes. Undeterred, I tap on the walls, listening if any sound different. Nothing. The second gong rings. I feel Karen pacing anxiously at the thought of being late, but I know it's here. My tapping continues, but the walls all sound the same. Defeated, I decide to try again later. I swivel my head from side to side. Where's Karen? My heart pounds, and I start to sweat. Karen peeks her head from inside the closet.

"It has a fake back. I saw it in a movie once." She smiles broadly.

I release a long, deep breath. Behind her is a passageway and a small stove. Yes! I'll come back with Honoré, a flash-light, and the evidence kit. We'll fingerprint the stove and see where the passage leads.

I wink at Karen, who smiles. The fingerprints on the stove

and possibly in the passageway will reveal who's involved. It's key to solving this. I feel it.

Hurriedly we head to our bedroom and change. Once in the hall, we see Honoré and Michelle. I need to place the stove into evidence and process it.

I whisper to Karen, "Take Michelle to the dining room. I'm going to have Honoré help me."

"*Now?*" she asks.

"Yeah, before anything can happen to it," I snap.

We wait for Michelle and Honoré to join us. Karen slips her arm in Michelle's and starts down the stairs, chatting about how wonderful Michelle looks this evening.

I elbow Honoré.

He knits his eyebrows together. "What?"

I smile. "You still have some fingerprinting supplies in your evidence kit?"

He nods silently.

"Grab it, and let's go. I've got something to show you."

Michelle stops on the stairs, turns, and releases a strong, exasperated breath. "Dan, this can wait until after dinner. I am sure of that!"

Honoré holds up his hands. "*Ma chérie*, it is fine. We will hurry to have it done and join you at dinner." He walks toward their room.

Michelle sets her lips in a firm, straight line. Her eyes hold no humor. Karen nudges her, and she relents.

Kit in hand, Honoré joins me, and I start for Dante's room.

"Why are we here, my friend?"

"I have new evidence. I found the stove that I'm sure was

used to kill Dante. If we can pull prints, we may have our killer."

We enter the bedroom. I pull back the closet door and push on the back of it until it opens.

Honoré peers inside. "A secret passage!"

Using the flashlight on my phone, I illuminate the tunnel, then swing my light around wildly. The stove is gone.

CHAPTER 21

"No, no, *NO!* It was just here!" I yell.

Honoré stands motionless as I continue to look about as if the stove will reappear at any moment.

"We can follow this tunnel. The stove may still be here," he offers quietly. I nod. Honoré places his evidence kit on the floor and illuminates the flashlight on his phone. My head clears the rafters as they're a little more than six feet tall, but luckily, I'm not. I point my light at an angle to see where I'm stepping. Honoré is a shadowy figure ahead of me. I hear a dull thud, followed by "*Merde.*" This is when height is *not* an advantage in policing. He stops before I notice, and I bump into him.

"Sorry," I mumble.

He swings his light from side to side. It's a crossroads. A passage to either side as well as forward. He leans in one direction, steps back, then faces another direction before throwing up his hands and moving forward. I'm content with having Honoré be in the lead to wherever this opens to. I have no clue where in the house I am and would prefer to not show up somewhere embarrassing, such as someone's bathroom while occupied.

We're on an ever so slight decline until a wall blocks our path. Honoré pushes on it until it gives way. He pokes his head out tentatively and "umm" escapes his lips.

"What?" I ask, attempting to look past him.

"Kitchen" is his reply. I hear Marie scream. Apparently the two of us coming out of the wall scared her. She is yelling in French. Honoré answers in a soothing tone. She snaps a reply and leaves the room.

"She was not aware of the passageway," Honoré says flatly.

"We need to rethink where someone could be hiding and moving in and out of rooms unseen. We never did find the stove," I state.

Nodding, he suggests, "Let us join our wives as they may be worried. We can think of a plan to explore the other passageways later."

We enter the dining room, and Michelle and Karen jump up. Camille and Jules are also at the table. Dr. Virk is dining alone. Another migraine for Sue?

Karen grabs my arm and whispers, "Where have you two been? Wait, you're covered in cobwebs, so let me guess. You were following the passageway." She rolls her eyes at me.

"What passageway?" Michelle inquires, looking at Honoré.

"You were not aware that there are secret passageways behind the walls in this house?" he asks, returning her gaze.

She shakes her head. "*Non.* Papa never said, so I do not think he knows. I'd like to see them."

"We can explore later," Honoré insists.

A simplified buffet is set up. Chicken stew, warm rolls, salad, and an array of dessert slices. We fill our plates and return to the table. Light conversation flows; however, I'm not really listening. I can't seem to sit still and proceed to push most of my dinner around the plate.

"We need to speak to your father-in-law again," I state to Honoré.

Karen taps my shoulder. "I'm going to ask Dr. Virk if he knows if Sue is okay."

Michelle, Honoré, and I exit the dining room. Butler is coming down the stairs. I inquire about the passages. He claims to know of them and assures us they are used at Monsieur Bres' discretion only. He bows and walks to the kitchen.

We're about to head to Monsieur Bres' office when Karen catches up with us.

"Dan, I think we'd better check on Sue. Dr. Virk said that she didn't feel well and wanted to lie down before dinner, but when he stopped by her room, she never answered. He assumed she came down, but she's not here."

Hurriedly, we make our way up the stairs to Sue's room. Karen knocks and calls for her. Nothing. She bites her lip as she looks at me. I drop my head. *Please, not again.* I exhale a deep breath and slowly turn the knob, calling out as I do.

Cautiously, I open the door and walk forward. The room is dark. Honoré reaches past me, turning the overhead light on. We continue to move into the room until we see Sue. She's in bed, her eyes in a frozen stare and her hands clenched tight. She's dead. I stare at her in disbelief. Another victim! I'm aware of how vulnerable we are. A gasp from behind alerts me that Karen followed us in. I turn to her. She has her hand over her mouth with her gaze fixated on Sue's pale face. I spin

Karen around and gently propel her from the room. Once in the hall, Honoré and I release a collective sigh.

"I will get the evidence kit I left in Dante's room," Honoré says.

I check that Karen is okay. Honoré does the same for Michelle. Karen nods that she's fine, but I see the terror in her eyes. Michelle informs us that she's going to speak to her father. Karen decides to go with her. They'll inform Butler of what has occurred. I'm not sure how comfortable I am with that, but with everything that's happening, I can't come up with a better plan.

Honoré returns and proceeds to inventory the supplies he has left. "I hope this is the last scene we need to process. We will use up everything I have."

The routine is the same: photos of the scene, bag and tag anything that appears suspicious, place Sue's hands in bags and secure them. Butler's discreet cough informs us he's present with the cart and sheet to transport the body. We place the victim on the cart and begin to move toward the elevator when Dr. Virk approaches. His eyes focus on the draped sheet. Wide and wild, they search all of us, pleading.

"I do not understand. I spoke to her earlier today. She said she had a nagging headache and thought a nap would help. What happened? I need to examine her."

Honoré steps between him and the body and places his hand in front of Dr. Virk's chest. Dr. Virk slaps it away, looking at Honoré with defiance on his face.

"We can't allow any more foreign D.N.A.," I utter quietly.

Dr. Virk glares at me, turns on his heels, and stomps to his room, slamming the door behind him. I sigh. "I do not think I can keep doing this," Honoré snaps.

Butler is studying the floor during this uncomfortable exchange with occasional glances at me. I nod my head toward the elevator. We make our way to it and on to the wine cellar refrigerator. We place Sue next to the other victims, close the door behind us, then trudge back to the house.

"We need to catalog this evidence along with the pictures for when the local authorities arrive."

Honoré rubs his forehead with his fingertips. "*Oui.*"

"Is that all you're going to say?" I bark. "People are being murdered."

"I know! I was almost one of the victims." His face flushes deep red.

True. Someone tried to kill him, but I question the validity of the attempt. I plan on saying what I think. I plant my feet and cross my arms over my chest. "I think you know more than you're saying."

"You have no right to say that. I am a good policeman!" He balls his hands into fists at his side.

I take a step closer. "I have every right. I'm not sure my wife and I are getting off this rock alive! Are you protecting someone?"

"*Non.*" He closes his eyes and sighs.

Angrily, I state, "Fine. Let's just get this done." I'm mentally exhausted.

We again use the office printer to download the photos. No one else is in the room. We work without a word said between us, compiling all the information and evidence and carrying it to the winery refrigerator. It's getting crowded in there.

We make our way back to the office. Now Monsieur Bres is behind the desk. Michelle positions herself on the arm of his chair and asks about the passages. He acknowledges knowing about them. He enjoys the gothic feel they give the house and adds that he was considering having William Wright improve them with wired lighting.

"It's creepy to know that someone could be using them to commit these awful crimes. Why keep them a secret?" Karen asks.

He directs his gaze at her. "This weekend was meant to be a, as you say, a 'trial run' of a new business venture I am exploring. It would be hosting murder mystery or escape room weekends. Had this weekend been successful, I had hoped to allow Butler to run the venture. However, the sadness and death of this weekend makes that business idea impossible. I am no longer pursuing those ideas."

Michelle rubs her father's back. He melts at her affection. For her sake, and Honoré's, I hope he's not involved, but he needs to answer some hard questions. I plan to use what I've discovered in Butler's file.

I snap, "Oops, just another loss for Butler."

His eyes hold no warmth or curiosity.

I continue, "Butler has a history with more than one of your guests."

A smirk flits across his lips, which tells me he already knows what I know. Cameras in the office, maybe?

"*Oui*" is his only reply accompanied by an emotionless mask.

"Papa?"

His facial expression softens, and he drops his head. Michelle is the key to questioning him.

She squeezes his hand. "You must tell us about this. Too many people are dead. What do you know?"

Bres relents with a slight bow of his head. "Butler was working for the gentleman that hired William Wright to design and build the building that killed the people. One of those killed was the gentleman's son. The loss triggered a massive and fatal stroke in the man."

Monsieur Bres nods rhythmically as I speak but adds nothing. "Then the insurance policy on that fire that Dante reported as accidental and paid you millions was written by Butler's younger brother. The insurance company fired him, and he ended up committing suicide."

He cocks his head sideways at me. A cold stare. Just "business, nothing personal," or waiting to see what else I have?

Honoré shifts uncomfortably in his chair.

"And?" Monsieur Bres asks dryly.

"Drew Taylor ruined a younger chef. That chef was from Butler's village. Butler invested heavily in the restaurant of the local boy making good. Butler was ruined when it went out of business," I reply, waiting for him to fill in the silence, but he doesn't.

Honoré jumps in. "How does Butler play a role in Louis' death?"

I glare back, never taking my eyes off Bres. "Oh, Monsieur Bres doesn't want a homosexual son. It would be easy for Butler to push Louis into a vat or immobilize him, then put him in. Problem solved."

"Dan, this does not make sense. Why would Butler move Drew's body or kill Sue? What happened to Thomas Thomas? We have never found any evidence to suggest it is Butler and not someone else." Honoré shakes his head. "We will need to see what the crime lab says about the evidence when the authorities arrive."

"He has motive and opportunity. He must know how to efficiently use the passageways to make his way through the house without being seen. I think we need to question him like a suspect to find out what he knows about the other victims. He may provide a reason he killed them too," I retort.

"*Non!*" Honoré yells. "We agreed, no judgments, no naming suspects. We will give the evidence we have collected to the authorities. It is their job to find suspects."

"Stop!" Michelle screams. Monsieur Bres is clutching his chest.

"You have upset my papa! Papa, are you alright?" Tears pool in her eyes as she faces her father.

He pats her arm, reaches for a small pill container in his pocket, which he opens, removes a pill, and places it under his tongue.

Honoré silently holds up his hand. I step back from another angry reply. Karen pats my knee as I force myself to calm down and breathe deeply. I'm not convinced his symptoms are real.

"Papa, come upstairs. You need to lie down and rest." Michelle shoots a scowl in my direction. He complies as she helps him from his chair and toward the elevator.

Honoré runs his hands through his hair, forcing deep, long sighs out.

"I'm sorry," I mutter.

"Angina. It was diagnosed last year. It's been under control with medication and his improved lifestyle. Stress makes it worse."

Michelle yells over her shoulder, "Honoré, get Dr. Virk and come to Papa's room." Honoré hurries from the office.

Karen looks at me sympathetically.

"I never meant for any harm to come to him," I say.

"I know you didn't. I think we need to slow down. No one is going anywhere at this point because there hasn't been a break in the weather, so still no phones or internet. I'll talk to Michelle later," Karen responds.

I close my eyes and tilt my head back. Yes, I'm a detective, but did I cross the friend line? Honoré is right. I was the one who suggested no judgments and to let the local authorities handle it. Butler is stuck here as we all are. For now, I just need to keep Karen and myself safe and hope for the best.

Karen stands up. "We still need to put the evidence from Sue's death on the board. Let's head to the living room, and we can work on that. Maybe even have a couple of drinks."

Standing in front of the board in the living room, Karen puts Sue's name on it.

"That makes me sad. Who'd want to hurt Sue, and *why?*" Karen asks.

I cross my arms over my chest. "If the other deaths were personalized, what means would you use to kill a nurse?"

"The way she looked when we found her, it looked like she had a reaction to something. Maybe someone switched her medication for something lethal or tampered with it."

Karen writes out a card with the words "medication switch or poison" and places it under Sue's name. I look through the pictures on my phone. There are no pill bottles in any of the pictures. Not anywhere. Whatever it was, it's been removed.

I drum my fingers on the back of the couch until Karen reaches over and stops me.

"That's annoying," she states.

"Sorry," I say. "Is your phone charged?"

Karen knits her eyebrows together. "Yeah."

"Let's check for a secret passage in Sue's room."

Karen collects her phone from our room and joins me in Sue's. I push on the back of the closet. Nothing happens. I tap on the walls. They all sound the same. We move furniture but don't find anything. Karen has a faraway look in her eyes. I can tell the wheels are turning in her brain.

"What are you thinking?" I question.

"I find it odd that there's a passageway in Dante's room, but not Sue's. Go through the opening in Dante's room and head back this way. I'll knock on the wall. Hopefully, there's a way to get here. Maybe the door's locked on the other side."

"Will do." I enter the passageway in Dante's room, move forward to where Honoré and I found the crossroads, and move to the left. I hear knocking, but it's distorted, and I can't be sure where it's coming from. I continue forward.

CHAPTER 22

I follow the knocking until I get to the place I believe it's coming from. A metal bar across the door blocks the door in the closet, making access from inside the bedroom impossible. I remove it and pull the door toward me. Karen falls into me.

"Ugh," she utters. "You could have told me you were here."

"Sorry," I reply. "There's a bar that can be used to secure the door from inside the passageway."

She grabs my arm. "Let's see if there's an entrance to our room."

"That's a good idea. First, I want to mark the passageway and make a map. Where they start and finish, each room, things like that. I need markers, paper, and tape. I'm sure we can find what we need in the kitchen. I don't want to go through the office."

"What about including Honoré in this?"

I shake my head. "I want this between us, for now."

Marie is in the kitchen, chopping vegetables, when we enter.

"Do you remember the French words for paper and tape?" I ask Karen.

She cocks her head to one side. "Let me think." She closes her eyes, then looks at Marie. "*Pardon, papier, le plume et adhésif, s'il vous plaît?*"

"Did you ask for adhesive?"

"I know there's another word for tape, but I can't think of it now."

It must be close enough as Marie moves across the room to a desk drawer and pulls it open. She points to the interior without a word. It has what we need.

"*Merci, merci,*" Karen says. Marie nonchalantly nods and returns to her chopping.

We take paper, tape, and a marker, then return to Sue's room. I enter the passageway, and Karen marks.

"Dan, I'm going to our room next. I need to see if there's an entrance."

I orientate myself and walk through the hall that forms a "U" shape. The tapping increases as I progress. Cobwebs cross my face, and I instinctively wipe them away. The knocking is right where I'm standing. I lift the bar and peek into our closet.

"Hello, there. Come here often?" I say in a mock sexy voice.

"Once has been too often," she replies, dusting webs off my shoulders. "You're a mess."

"But a happy mess as it means no one's been down this way for a while."

Her eyes light up, and she smiles. It's a good thing.

I extend my hand. "Follow me, madame."

She switches on the flashlight on her phone and says in a little girl voice. "You just take me to the best places."

Karen fits in the passageway easily. My head clears the rafters, but barely, and I feel the need to hunch over. I know the room next to us belongs to Jules and Camille. The bar is in place, and I'm not about to open it. Karen notes it on the diagram. We return to the main aisle, and to the right is another small hall that dead-ends after it passes Dr. Virk's, then Honoré and Michelle's room. Loud, angry words in French permeate the wall. Michelle says my name and words like "*imbecile*" and "*stupide*." None of this sounds good for me. I have a feeling of dread that my actions in Monsieur Bres' office led to this. Remorse washes over me as Honoré is subjected to the verbal assault. I step back from the door quietly and return to the main hall. We work our way back toward Sue's room.

First, I find Thomas Thomas' room. It's been cleaned. I doubt he's coming back. Next, William Wright's is in the same condition. The third door has the bar removed. I push the door open slowly and recognize it as Dante's. I bolt inside and spin in circles. Horrified! The bed linens are stripped off, the mattress left bare, surfaces wiped, and all evidence of our crime scene processing gone. I hurriedly return to the passageway and check on Drew Taylor's. It too is spotless. I'm freaked out. This will negatively impact the investigations. Karen finishes the diagram. We realize that the passageways run behind the faux fireplaces and mantels.

There is a slight incline on each of the three main passageways that form the "U." There is the one that Honoré and I found going to the kitchen. Another leads to the living room, hidden behind a bookcase. Very murder mystery-ish. The last opens to the dining room. *That's* how Monsieur Bres seemed to "disappear" from the room.

We step out of the passageway and into Sue's room. My mind is reeling. Who would have cleaned up the rooms, and is the evidence locked in the winery refrigerator still there? I debate on involving Honoré, but then he holds the key.

Karen involuntarily shudders. "This is creepy."

"Creepier than several people dying?" I ask.

She releases an exasperated sigh. "No, but you know what I mean. How do we know if someone will try and get into our room while we're sleeping?"

"I'm going to make sure I know if they do now."

"How?"

I wink at her. She follows me out of the bedroom, into the hall, and down to the dining room. No one else is in the room. I find several wine glasses. We each take six and head back upstairs. In the closet, I place the glasses side by side in two rows in front of the secret door. No one will see them in the dark, and they won't be able to miss knocking them over. I'll hear that.

The dressing gong sounds. Karen and I dress casually, both of us in black pants and white shirts. Karen adds a black cardigan. We start down the stairs. The faint sound of hushed voices in the hall below catches my attention. I peer over the railing. Camille is there, near the kitchen door. I see her head and shoulders. Her companion is obscured from sight. I press my finger to my lips, signaling for Karen to be quiet while we descend, hoping to hear what is said.

"Tonight, yes! We must end him!" she hisses vehemently in English. This seems a strong statement for Camille, who has appeared more passive-aggressive than outright aggressive thus far this weekend.

Her companion mumbles something in reply. I can't discern who the other voice belongs to or if it's male or female.

I'm about to make the curve on the stairs that gives me a clear view of the hall when Honoré calls to Karen and me. I wince.

When I check the hall, no one is there, not even Camille. Butler swings the kitchen door open and moves toward me with a platter of vegetables.

He bows slightly. "Good evening, sir, madame."

"Excuse me." I hold up a finger to stop him.

He stops walking and raises his eyebrows, silently asking, "Yes?"

"I thought I heard someone talking in the hall, but they seem to have disappeared. Did anyone come into the kitchen just now?"

"No, sir. Marie and I have been preparing dinner. I did not see anyone else. Is there something you need, sir?"

I wave him off. "No, no. Just curious. Thank you."

He gives another snap of his head before continuing toward the dining room. Curiouser and curiouser. I saw Camille and heard another person, but where oh where could they be? Karen and I didn't find an entrance from the hall to the passageway. If someone did go into the kitchen, why would Butler lie . . . unless he was the other person. He has motive and means. What did Camille mean by "Tonight, we must end him" and who's "he"? My anxiety is rising. I don't want yet another death. Camille can inherit as Jules' widow. Maybe he's the "he." Butler did appear shortly after Camille and the other person vanished. If he's her companion, then he was perfectly situated to step into the kitchen, grab the platter, and return to the hall.

Honoré and Michelle join us as we enter the dining room. They too have a more relaxed attire of pants and sweaters.

Camille walks in just as we sit down. She's wearing a short, white lace dress. It adheres to her rolls of fat, and its seams appear strained. Dr. Virk is, as always, perfectly tailored in dress pants and a crisp, gray shirt. Both approach the buffet. Dr. Virk bows and steps aside for Camille to be first. Oddly, she giggles and pats his arm. He pulls it away like her touch hurts. A look of sadness flits across Camille's face. What's going on? Is he who she was talking to, but why would Dr. Virk be part of killing anyone? Is she looking for romance with the eligible doctor, or a weekend fling? He looks around. Our eyes meet, and he flushes scarlet, then breaks eye contact. It doesn't appear as if he's interested in Camille.

Monsieur Bres and Jules are absent. I hope both are alright. My guess is Monsieur Bres is resting after the incident in his office earlier today, but Jules, where's he? I need to stop asking that question as the answer is never good. Camille sits at Dr. Virk's table. He approaches our table, looks over both shoulders, leans closer to us, and whispers, "Any update on who is doing these killings?"

I shake my head.

Anger flashes in his eyes. "Well, hurry up and figure it out. I do not want to narrow the suspect pool by being a victim," he snaps, walking to a table, but not the one he was occupying earlier where Camille is sitting at now. She looks after him longingly.

Karen and I join Honoré and Michelle. I need to see how upset she is with me. "Michelle, I'm sorry about upsetting your father."

Michelle stares at me for a couple of seconds as if choosing her words before replying. "Thank you for that, but you were wrong to accuse him of anything to do with these bad things. He invited you to his home as his guest. This is not how you treat your host. I want you to stop." She stands and makes her way to the buffet. Karen, Honoré, and I follow.

On the buffet sits a platter of vegetables along with hummus, roasted chicken, fresh rolls, steamed broccoli, pureed strawberries, and meringue shells accompanied by a bowl of whipped cream. Butler weaves his way around tables with bottles of white wine or sparkling water. Karen and I opt for water. Wine no longer entices me. We eat in silence. Karen attempts to start a conversation about the continued heavy rains and asks anyone to speculate on it ending, but neither Honoré nor Michelle seem interested. Michelle eats quickly and excuses herself to check on her father.

Honoré sits back at the table. "She is worried about him."

A wave of guilt floods me, causing me to drop my shoulders and release a deep breath. "I'm sorry if I caused any damage with my accusations." I hold his stare.

He rests his face on his fists under his chin, softly nodding until he rubs his hands over his face. "I just don't know."

"Don't know what?" I ask.

"Who to believe. Who to trust. Why these people? Why this weekend? If someone wanted them dead, they could have killed them years ago. None of the things they are accused of happened recently. Come with me to look at the board again."

Karen and I trudge behind him to the living room. He stands in front of the murder board. I'm waiting for him to have some revelation as to the reason we're doing this again. None comes.

"I hate this. What to do next . . ." he throws out more as a statement.

"Question Butler," I say more forcefully than I intended.

Honoré leans forward and knits his eyebrows together questioningly.

"He needs to answer for the information I found in his file."

"Did you go through my father-in-law's private papers?"

I glare back at him. "Not the point right now. Butler has had opportunity all weekend, knows about the passageways, and now I found motive. That leads a good investigator to question a suspect. I tried questioning Monsieur Bres, and that didn't work. So, either you're part of this or you're not."

Honoré winces at my mention of questioning his father-in-law. "*Oui.* You are right. Let us talk to him now."

The three of us head for the kitchen. Marie is absent from the room. We corner Butler as he dries wine glasses at the sink. In full proper English butler form, he stands very upright and addresses us. "Is there something you need?"

Honoré looks at me and then studies the floor. Apparently, I'm lead detective on this.

I clear my throat. Butler turns his gaze to me.

"It has come to my attention that you have a connection to most, if not all, of our victims," I start.

His face holds no readable emotion. "I'm not sure I understand that statement, sir." His gaze is unwavering.

I don't break eye contact. "Well, let me lay it out. First, there's Drew Taylor, who ruined the restaurant of a young chef that you had heavily invested in. Then there was William Wright. His company's poor construction killed your last employer's son and contributed to that man's sudden death. Dante Fuoco's fabricated report that a business fire was accidental caused the insurance company to pay millions in damages and cost your brother his job since he sold the policy. What do you have to say for yourself?"

"Sir, I'm offended that you believe I would cause the demise of these people."

"You invited them," I point out.

He answers without any change in emotion, "At the discretion of my current employer."

"How do you account for having a history with so many of the victims?"

"I don't. I was aware of Mr. Taylor and his disgrace, but not the others. To my knowledge they would have worked for companies. I would not have known their individual names. As for Ms. Jensen, I have not been to Canada or utilized Dr. Virk's practice. I have no motive for her death."

I doubt the truth of his statements but have no evidence to connect him to these murders. I push further. "What about Louis' relationship with Jules. Monsieur Bres didn't approve. Would you have killed for him?"

Butler's voice catches. "I . . . I . . . ." He gulps a reply. I feel Karen's hand on my arm, pulling me. I look at her, but she's focused on Butler.

"You loved Louis, didn't you?" she asks softly. Butler blinks several times in rapid succession, then nods.

Karen moves into social worker mode. "Can you tell me about him?"

Butler draws in a ragged breath. "He made time on this

isolated rock bearable." A sob follows. I want to yell "Stop!" at opening this man's emotional pain. Karen reaches for Butler's hand and gently squeezes it.

"He was kind and funny." A smile crosses his lips as he speaks.

"But not monogamous?" Karen probes Butler's eyes. A love triangle would give him motive. If I can't have him, no one will.

"No. Louis was not," he croaks out, sucking in deep breaths, "but having some of him was better than being with-out him totally." His body spasms with choking cries. Karen wraps her arms around him. Butler's back stiffens for a few minutes until he releases a deep sigh, sniffles, then regains his composure. "I apologize for my unprofessional display. I can assure you all that I had nothing to do with the deaths that have occurred here. I hope you believe me."

Karen rubs Butler's back. "We'll leave you to it. I'm sorry we intruded into your private life. Please forgive us." He gives a weak smile.

We file out of the kitchen.

"That was awkward," Honoré states.

I run my hand through my hair. I was so sure I was right about Butler. The suspect pool is narrowing, but they may not be who we think.

Honoré bids us good night and walks up the stairs.

I wrestle with the thought of telling him about the clean rooms and asking if we should check on the evidence locked in the winery but decide to end this day.

CHAPTER 23

I toss and turn in bed, convinced I hear wine glasses being disturbed in our closet. After checking them several times and finding nothing, I fall into an unsettled sleep. Karen startles awake next to me.

"You okay?" I ask.

She sits up, pushes her hair behind her ears, and replies, "Yeah. I had the weirdest dream. I was holding Thomas' hand as he slipped over the edge of a cliff. I heard a scream. I couldn't get to him. That's when I woke up."

I hold her close. Her dreams can be insightful. Unfortunately, this one reinforces the theory that Thomas slipped, fell, or was pushed off the mountainside. Another victim! Is the killer done, or are others still at risk?

"Look!" Karen screeches.

"What?" Another shot of adrenaline hits me.

Karen smiles at me as she points to the window. "That's called sunshine. No rain, no gray clouds. Just beautiful blue skies and sun. We should be able to call for help and get out of here."

Karen jumps up. We waste no time in getting dressed and head down the stairs. Honoré is at the bottom.

I grasp his hand. "Did you see it, my friend?" His broad smile has returned.

"*Oui*, the sun has returned. I will work with my father-in-law to reach the authorities. Hopefully, we will be rescued by the end of the day."

"That would be great. One thing first. I'd like to check the evidence in the winery refrigerator to be sure it's all cataloged correctly for when they arrive."

"We will have much explaining to do. We can go after breakfast." Michelle joins us.

Everything seems better today. The shadows of the house have retreated, and people talk more positively. I grab a cup of coffee that slides down my throat, smooth and delicious.

Monsieur Bres sits at our table. Michelle coos and fusses over him until he waves her off. She fills a plate and places it in front of him.

Butler moves from table to table with jugs of water and juice, filling glasses. Karen and I head to the buffet. Scrambled eggs, slices of cheese, ham, warm rolls, butter, jam, and slices of melon are laid out.

Back at the table, Honoré and Michelle are speaking rapidly in French to Monsieur Bres, who nods as he eats. I catch the words "gendarmeries," "homicide," "corps," "suspecter." True to his word, Honoré is discussing reaching out to the local police.

We finish breakfast. Honoré stands. "Dan, my father-in-law will do what he can to send a message to the authorities and explain what has happened. He will let me know as soon as he speaks to them. Let us check on the evidence."

I feel a bounce in my step as we head to the winery. Honoré seems taller this morning. At the refrigerator door, Honoré extracts the key from his pocket. The door swooshes open, and a blast of cold air escapes. We step inside and *freeze*, both physically and figuratively. Nothing's there! No evidence bags, no bodies, nothing but wooden crates filled with bottles of wine.

Honoré's eyes look around wildly as he spins in place. "*Merde*."

"Well put," I snap.

"I . . . but . . . I . . . when . . . locked . . ." Honoré stammers and searches the room as if the evidence has hidden itself.

"And that's not all. Our victims' rooms have been stripped and cleaned."

"*Non* . . . why?"

"Destroy the evidence, hard to prosecute," I say, looking at him incredulously.

He's staring blankly as if plumbing his mind for an explanation. I rub my fingertips across my forehead. Theories, motives, suspects, and what to do next run through my brain.

"We're going to have to confront your father-in-law. This didn't just *happen*. Someone is orchestrating everything that's happened this weekend."

"This is wrong. We will go now," he says, looking up. He utters, "Please forgive me, Michelle."

Both of us march with purpose to the elevator. Honoré mutters in French, under his breath, the whole ride. I formulate a line of questioning that will be pursued with or without chest pain on the part of Monsieur Bres.

The elevator opens on the third floor. Honoré knocks on

the door to Monsieur Bres' suite. No answer. He knocks again, much harder. Still nothing. I turn the doorknob and open the door.

It's completely dark inside. I grope for a light switch on the wall and flip it on to illuminate the room. No one, no sound, and no movement.

Honoré slaps my shoulder. "The office," he says, turning on his heels. I follow him to the elevator. Once inside, Honoré is pacing and talking to himself. I hope *he* doesn't have a heart attack.

He strides through the open doors. I quicken my step to keep up. He doesn't bother to knock before entering the office, but stops so suddenly, I bounce off his shoulder. His head swivels from side to side.

"No one is here. Where can he be?" Honoré asks, sounding puzzled.

Oh no! Whenever we can't find someone, it doesn't end well.

Butler steps into the room. He seems surprised to find us here.

"Where is the *patron*?" Honoré inquires.

"I was under the impression he was in here, sir."

"Well, he is not, and he's not in his suite or in the winery," Honoré states. "We will search the house."

I close my eyes. This feels like we've dealt with this scenario before. I'm not sure I can face another victim; however, I fall in line behind Honoré as he heads toward the dining room, the living room, and finally the kitchen. No Monsieur Bres. Back in the hall, we're joined by Karen and Michelle. Honoré asks Michelle if she has seen her father since breakfast.

"*Oui*, Papa is touring the vineyards to assess how much damage all the rain has caused."

I jump in. "He's not dead. That's good. Was he able to reach the authorities?"

"He was not, but said he will try again later."

"We can ourselves." I look directly at Honoré.

Honoré says, "Monsieur Bres will do his best. We can also try later."

Karen lays her hand on Michelle's arm. "Is he well enough to walk the whole way?"

Michelle laughs. "He does not walk. He takes a golf cart and was excited to get outside. I am not worried as Dr. Virk is with him. Camille told me he is going to the fire pit to burn bags of trash."

Why is *he* doing it? He has staff to do these things. I suddenly realize it could be trash or *evidence*! We need to find him, now!

"Where's the fire pit?" I say more forcefully than I intend.

Michelle pauses. "I am not sure. Butler must know. I will ask."

I want to scream "Hurry!" but instead I take a couple of deep breaths. She checks the kitchen. Butler is there. The four of us proceed back to the kitchen. He explains that the fire pit is located approximately one hundred yards in front of the helipad, but he has never known the master to dispose of trash himself.

Honoré looks at me. "Why would Camille say he was out burning trash? Has anyone seen her this morning?" All heads shake no.

"Neither Camille nor Dr. Virk were at breakfast. I assumed they'd come down later, but what if one or both are . . ." Karen's voice trails off without finishing the thought.

Michelle remains in the kitchen, pouring herself a cup of coffee as Honoré, Karen, and I race upstairs to Camille and Jules' bedroom. I knock firmly. Jules pulls open the door.

"Is Camille with you?" I question, rather out of breath.

He looks between Honoré, Karen, and me. "No, she said she had work to do in the office and went there."

Honoré and I exchange glances. We know she's not there. I rack my brain to try and figure out what's going on. It's like everyone is on the move with nowhere to go. We check Dr. Virk's room. It's been cleaned, and his personal things have been removed. This is not a good omen. If he's a victim, where is his body?

"Dan, we need to start finding people and bring them to the kitchen," Honoré says as he moves toward the stairs. I take Karen's hand and start walking in the same direction.

Honoré stops in the middle of the hall. "What is that?"

"What are you looking at?" I ask. He points out the window. There is an enormous fire. Flames shoot high into the air. All of us scramble down the stairs. I ask Karen to stay inside with Michelle, especially if it's a body being burned. Honoré and I race through the kitchen into the garage for a golf cart. Honoré floors the gas pedal, but these machines weren't built for speed. If my knees were better, I think I could outrun it. After what seems like an inordinately long time, we reach the fire. Surprise overtakes me. Camille is throwing our evidence bags into the flames.

Jumping out of the cart, I scream, "What are you doing?"

She turns with a vicious smile and locks eyes on me. "It is all gone. You cannot prove anything." Laughing, she tosses the final bag in to be incinerated.

Honoré bails out of the cart and attempts to retrieve items from the flames, but the heat is too much. He's forced to step back. I grab Camille.

There's not much that can be done to save our evidence. Camille struggles and swears in French. Honoré holds her by the shoulders and questions her. Only a grunt escapes her.

"Dan, I will walk her back to the house if you drive the cart. I have nothing to restrain her with."

Camille makes spontaneous remarks. "You are both so *stupide*. You never guessed that he is making his revenge on bad people who hurt him. Now the proof is gone. He loves me and will come get me."

"Who's he?" I inquire.

She turns to me with a malicious grin and wiggles in place as she begins to hum. If she's making a case for temporary insanity, it might work.

I feel extremely tired as if this weekend will never end. A weird whirling sound catches my attention. The three of us turn toward the helipad. Camille bites Honoré's hand. He pulls it away, letting go of her with a yelp. She starts running toward the sound. We're in pursuit. The helicopter is in sight. There's a person in the pilot's seat, but I can't make out who until I'm closer. It's Dr. Virk. The helicopter blades are in motion, and it lifts off. He makes eye contact with me and gives a mock salute before flying away.

"*Non, mon amour. Attends-moi . . . je t'aime, non*," Camille wails and sobs. She runs toward where the helicopter was, then trips and falls to the ground in a weeping ball. The copter continues without hesitation until it's out of sight.

Honoré has his hands on top of his head. I'm speechless. Camille is face down in the grass, weeping uncontrollably. My shoes are wet. There's an earthy scent assaulting my nose. A chill runs through me. Honoré and I help Camille to her feet and slowly make our way back to the golf cart. She slumps in the seat, resigned, and offers no resistance as we drive back to the house. We trudge inside the kitchen. Camille is softly crying. She wipes her face with the back of her hand.

In the kitchen, I set Camille in a chair, then Honoré and I each drop into one. I don't know if I should cry, have a drink, or cry while having a drink. This doesn't make sense. Dr. Virk was low on my suspect list. How is he connected to these guests? What did Camille mean by "He's making his revenge on bad people?" Monsieur Bres knowingly allowed a murderer to carry out his evil plan in his home, but how else were these particular people invited? I'm missing something. Michelle and Karen join us at the table.

Honoré summarizes what happened. Silence falls over the room. Marie quietly hands each of us a cup of hot coffee. The deep, black brew warms me as I'm lost in my thoughts of reaching the authorities.

"What's that sound?" Michelle asks.

Absentmindedly, I ask, "What?" Before I finish my question, I hear it. The sound of a helicopter. I'm on full alert. Has Dr. Virk returned? Is he armed? I scan the room for weapons.

Knives are the best I can find. I'm formulating an attack plan if it is Dr. Virk.

Moments later, joy rushes over me. Three local police officers and Thomas Thomas on crutches ambulate toward the house. We're rescued.

Honoré, Karen, Michelle, and I rush out to greet them. The sight of our group running at them causes the officers to stop and place their hands on their holsters. Honoré puts his hands up, then reaches slowly for his wallet out of his back pant pocket and shows them his badge. We're ushered back into the house. French is being spoken very rapidly. Honoré translates, indicating that we should gather in the dining room to answer questions. Karen hugs Thomas so hard that he begins to lose his balance, but she grabs hold until he's stable. We sit at tables. Butler, Marie, and Jules join us. Where is Monsieur Bres?

CHAPTER 24

In the dining room, Honoré and the officers shake hands and make introductions; however, it's all in French. I'm left out.

Karen is questioning Thomas about what happened to him.

He smiles. "I took the climbing gear to rappel down the side of the mountain but miscalculated the amount of rope I needed and dropped about twenty feet, breaking my ankle. That slowed my getting to town and the local authorities."

I should never doubt Karen's dreams. Thomas was brought back by the authorities as he is still a suspect and needs to go through his thoughts of what occurred in the house.

Honoré announces that Inspector LeGrand will conduct the investigation. He's a tall, thin man with sharp facial features and a nose that overpowers his face. Dark, penetrating eyes. No smile. Two young, fresh-faced uniform officers stand on either side of the door at attention.

I notify Honoré that Monsieur Bres is missing. He lays a hand on Michelle's shoulder. "Where is your papa?"

"He is resting in his suite."

Marie says something. Honoré motions for me to go with him. The inspector snaps something, and one of the officers follows us.

"Where are we going?" I ask.

Honoré calls over his shoulder, "The winery. Marie noticed my father-in-law and Dr. Virk walking that way this morning."

I silence any comments I have. The passageway feels longer than it has in the past. There we check the vat room, the refrigerator, and the bottling room. No one.

Honoré throws up his hands and scowls. I'm tired of these searches that yield nothing. We start back to the house when the thought occurs to me that we haven't checked Louis' room. I debate letting it go, but just can't. At the door to his room, I try the knob. It's locked.

"Did you secure this?" I question Honoré.

"*Non.*"

I step to one side and knock, then listen intently. A chair scrapes the floor. I hear what sounds like a whimper. I step back and ram my shoulder into the door. It doesn't move. Honoré joins in, and it gives way. My eyes adjust to the low light.

Monsieur Bres is bound to a chair. His head hangs down, and a low moan escapes his lips. We rush to him. Honoré unties him while I survey his injuries. He has a bleeding lower lip, and his left eye is swollen shut. Gently, we remove him from the chair and lay him on the bed.

Honoré speaks to him. He mutters a response.

"What's he saying? Who did this? When did this happen?" I question.

"Dr. Virk" is his singular reply.

Monsieur Bres sits up with Honoré's help.

"We will get him to the house," Honoré states.

I place Monsieur Bres' arm around my neck. Honoré is on

the other side. We begin a slow pace to the kitchen. The young officer is speechless and follows behind us.

In the kitchen, we place him in a chair. Honoré grabs a towel, reaches into the freezer, and places ice into the towel.

He holds the pack in front of Monsieur Bres. "*Patron*, for your oeil or lèvre, or . . ." His voice trails off.

Monsieur Bres places it over his eye. Karen and Michelle enter the kitchen. Michelle races to her father's side. The inspector enters the room, and orders are given. The officer that accompanied us is giving his report. It looks the same in any language. LeGrand's eyes rove over each of us but give nothing away.

Everyone is directed back to the dining room, including Monsieur Bres. Once there, we sit at one table. LeGrand uses the office as an interview room. I'm a bit put out that he's taken over the investigation, but it is his jurisdiction.

One by one, each of us is called to give our account of what occurred here. Honoré is the first, then me. I mention that I don't speak or understand French. A sly smile creases the inspector's lips. "I studied at an American university."

I laugh out loud. "Excellent." I recount my experience since arriving. He nods intermittently but never comments. Direct questions are asked and answered. He scratches words in a notebook, occasionally underlining items. All routine for me. He takes my phone, reviews the photos, and tags it for evidence.

The final person to be questioned is Camille. She sobs, sneezes, coughs, and her nose drips. She draws in ragged breaths as she's accompanied by LeGrand toward the office. She stops, pulls a rescue inhaler from her pocket, charges it, and draws a breath from it. She coughs hard. She takes a second draw, then gags and drops to the floor. I jump up. Karen is right behind me. I kneel next to her to give C.P.R. and mouth to mouth when Karen grabs my shirt and pulls me back.

"Dan, stop!" she shouts.

"What?" I demand sharply.

"Bitter almonds. I can smell it," she replies.

I rear back. I can't smell anything. Camille is pale, her lips blue and eyes open. Clearly, she's dead. LeGrand takes charge. A perimeter is set, and we're directed to the far side of the room. The inhaler is placed in an evidence bag and photos are taken. Another victim. I hold Karen close as she cries silently into my shoulder.

Honoré and LeGrand confer. We are questioned with regards to Camille and access to the inhaler. LeGrand announces that Camille's body will be removed for autopsy and asks that we be patient as arrangements to have us removed from the mountain will take time. LeGrand collects passports from each of us. He announces that our luggage will be searched before we leave the grounds. Karen and I head upstairs. I've never been happier at the thought of a vacation coming to an end.

"Karen, be sure to check each item before you pack. I don't want any surprises, like someone placing something incriminating in a pocket," I say.

First we both inspect our suitcases for any contraband. Slowly and methodically, each item is laid out, gone over, when possible turned inside out, and packed. When we're satisfied that no one has tampered with any of our belongings, we close our cases.

"We need to retain possession of these at all times. Never leave the bags unattended."

"Okay," Karen replies quietly. "I just want to get out of here."

I know that everything that's happened has upset her. We head downstairs. Honoré meets us in the hall and informs me that LeGrand has sent the two officers to escort Camille's body to the helicopter and then to the medical examiner. The helicopter can accommodate four people and luggage. Several trips will be made. The second trip includes Jules, Marie, Butler, and Thomas.

"Shouldn't Monsieur Bres go first and see a doctor for his injuries?" I ask.

He shakes his head. "He's refused. He insists others go before him. Michelle will go with him in the helicopter. We will all be detained at the police station until our formal statements are typed and signed. LeGrand has insisted that everyone remain in the area until the inquest is concluded and a ruling made."

Karen and I drag our luggage to the living room and sit down to wait our turn to leave.

Karen points. "Dan, can we dump our murder board? I'm so sad at all the death that has occurred," she says.

Silently, I walk over to the board, take it down, and turn it to face the wall behind where we're sitting. Honoré joins us.

I make eye contact with him. "How's Jules doing?"

He releases a long, deep sigh. "I don't know. I have no words to ease his pain. He has lost two people close to him this weekend."

I follow up. "And Michelle?"

He scratches his head. I see fear reflected in his eyes. "Using her father as an excuse to keep busy. Karen, can you check in with her? She doesn't want to leave him alone but needs to pack. He'll be in his suite until it is time to leave."

"I'll go up now," Karen states, leaving the suitcases with me. Honoré moves to the bar and the remaining alcohol. "I need a drink or two," he scoffs.

He starts mixing the remains of various bottles in a pitcher. I'm a bit anxious at what this cocktail will be. When he's satisfied, he pours each of us a glass. My first sip isn't bad for a gin, vodka, rum something.

"Just between the two of us, I *never* want to come here again. I am sorry, my friend, for how this experience was for you and Karen." Sadness and regret fill his eyes.

Guilt washes over me for suspecting my friend of these horrible murders. An idea strikes me. "We need to get out of here so you and Michelle can show Karen and me the France you love. Agreed?"

He brightens up. "*Oui!*"

We sip our cocktails and make plans. He has a list of places to go. I remind him to confer with my social director/travel agent Karen to be sure their lists are compatible.

LeGrand steps into the room. He informs me that Karen and I will be on the next helicopter with Michelle and Monsieur Bres. Honoré and LeGrand will be the last to leave to secure the scene for the forensic team.

Nervous excitement brews in my stomach. I envision Karen and me sitting next to each other watching this awful rock disappear behind us as we make our way to town. Once we land, we need to contact our son to let him know we're okay. Just the thought of saying "We're okay" brings me joy.

Honoré and I are well into our third drink when LeGrand says that the helicopter will be here shortly. I gather the luggage and step into the hall as Karen comes down the stairs. Michelle and Monsieur Bres are behind her. She takes her cases from me. Stress lines show on her face, her eyes are distant, and her lips are tightly pursed.

I lean closer to her. "Is everything alright?"

She pats my arm and forces a smile as Michelle and her father join us.

LeGrand escorts us to the helipad. Moments later, the helicopter lands. We load our luggage, then ourselves on board. LeGrand closes the door and signals to the pilot to take off. I feel as if I'm abandoning Honoré there.

Karen snuggles into my arm. She shivers. Now I'm more concerned about what's going on with her.

The trip takes mere minutes for us to land and arrive inside the station. Odd how being cut off made it feel much further away and escape unattainable. The sun is out. I hear cars and voices. I'm thrilled that Karen and I are here. We're directed inside, separated, and questioned regarding the events of the weekend. Each of us has an officer fluent in English. Formal statements are taken. When typed up, we're asked to read them over and sign them.

Karen asks for directions to a local hotel. One of the officers suggests a family-run inn nearby. We walk there, luggage and all. Michelle and her father join us. With her help, we're able to secure a room. Michelle books another for her father as well as one for Honoré and herself.

Our room is simply decorated with one bed, a small nightstand, and two wooden chairs, but it couldn't be any better if it were The Ritz. Relief at being here with Karen rushes through me like electricity. Every muscle in my body relaxes. We call our son, Eric. It's good to hear his voice. He wants details of why he hasn't heard from us before this. We explain the lack of communication due to the terrain and weather. We'll talk more face-to-face.

I hang up and glance over at Karen. The tears stream down her face. I gather her in my arms, and we stand quietly for a few moments. She pushes away from me, dabs her eyes, and says, "I need to tell you something. I know who the murderer is."

"It's Dr. Virk, right?"

"Yes and no." She sighs. "He killed Sue. He had a patient that wronged his family. He purposely let the patient die. Sue knew Dr. Virk's secret, lied for him, and blackmailed him for years."

"Wow, what a jerk."

"There's more. I confronted Monsieur Bres when we were alone this afternoon. He acknowledged it was his plan, although he didn't carry out any of the actual killing himself."

I stammer, search for words, and bark out, "But all the information on Butler. He must have been involved too."

"Monsieur Bres planted some and contorted some to fit the narrative for you to find. He gambled on the idea you would investigate with or without Honoré."

I'm pacing around the room, trying to comprehend this.

"Why?" That's the best I can come up with. I drop into one of the chairs.

Karen sits next to me. "This is the explanation. Monsieur Bres is dying from liver cancer. It's beyond any treatment, hence his yellowish hue. He tried to cover it up by tanning. He wants to right some of his and others' wrongdoings. He helped Drew Taylor ruin the young chef, bribed officials to cover up William Wright's poor construction, and paid Dante Fuoco handsomely to torch the building and write a favorable report so insurance could be claimed."

"That is some messed-up ethics. Who did the actual killing?" I ask hesitantly.

"Dr. Virk and Camille. Virk was paid three million euros and given a new identity for his part and a means to escape. It was Camille's idea to tie up Bres. She feared he wouldn't allow their escape. Virk assisted, but Camille did the actual hitting for the 'years of verbal abuse from Monsieur Bres.' They moved the bodies to a hole that was recently dug. I'm sure they'll be found."

My mouth drops open. "Camille? I don't get it."

"Monsieur Bres doesn't miss much, especially when he installed cameras everywhere. He knew about Jules being gay and his affair with Louis. He told Dr. Virk, who flattered Camille, made promises, and played on her sense of loyalty when he told her the victims were 'bad people' and were out to destroy him. Dr. Virk poisoned the candy for Drew and Sue's medication, but Camille delivered them. He also poisoned her inhaler."

"What about the cabinet that fell on William Wright?"

"Virk removed the bolts and placed the heater in Dante's room through the secret passage."

"Louis?"

"Camille on her own. It just happened to be ironic that he drowned in wine." She shrugs. "She also tried to kill Jules in the living room by putting rat poison in his drink, but he didn't drink it, and I knocked it out of his hand. That's why she insisted on cleaning up the broken glass."

"But Butler gave out the clues. He must have known."

Karen shakes her head. "Bres gave the instructions, and Butler did as he was told. Oh, yeah, Bres wanted Honoré dead. He believes Honoré was never good enough for Michelle. Dr. Virk's clue appeared to take him outside. Once there, he entered the garage, started the cars, waited for Honoré, and locked him in."

I squeeze my hands open and closed as rage surges through me. How dare Monsieur Bres feel the right to do this. I want to find him and drag him by the collar to the police.

Karen reads my thoughts and hugs me. "He's going to confess everything at the inquest. He wants time to explain to Michelle first. He assures me that we were never in danger. I'm not convinced of that."

"I would pay money to see him in a jail cell," I snap.

"He's not going to jail."

"If he confesses, then why not?"

"His Plan A is, and I quote, 'I have very good lawyers, and rich men don't go to prison.' He hopes to stall long enough to die before going to jail. Plan B is the ring he plays with on his hand. It's a Borgia poison ring. There's a small compartment that hides a cyanide capsule."

I'm overwhelmed with an array of emotions. Anger,

sadness, exhaustion, joy at being free. Facing Honoré and Michelle will be difficult. I know Michelle's heart will be broken. Karen and I sit for a long time, silent and still. The light of the day fades outside our window. This is one 'aventure' we'll never forget and hope to never repeat. For now, having Karen with me and knowing we're safe is enough. Tomorrow will bring a new day. I'll deal with it then.